CHRISTMAS at MANORDALE

A Jack France Mystery

By

Margaret Holbrook

Manordale, the estate of Jack France is in Moretondale and is part of Melford District. Melford is the nearest town.

Christmas at Manordale

October 1928

'I was hoping for a carol service this year at St. Stephen's but I don't know whether we'll be able to have one. There's no news of the new vicar arriving yet, or I haven't heard of it if there is. Mr France might know of course but I think I should be told if he knows anything. After all I am the churchwarden,' Mrs Price said to her husband as they sat together in the sitting room of their small cottage.

'I'm sure you'll know soon enough,' Hubert Price replied. These things take time. They always do. And you never know, something might come up that means we can organise something at the church. I'm sure Mr France wouldn't object, in fact, I think he'd encourage you, were you to mention it to him.'

'Do you really think so?' Eileen asked.

'Yes, I do,' Mr Price replied.

Mrs Price smiled. 'You're a good man Hubert Price,' she said , 'and . . .' the telephone began to ring and interrupted their conversation. Mrs Price went into the small hall of their cottage to answer it. 'Hello,' she said, as she picked up the receiver. A voice answered her greeting. Mrs Price didn't reply for a moment or two and then she asked, 'Is that you, Richard?'

When Mrs Price returned to the sitting room the smile that had graced her lips only a few minutes earlier had now vanished. She looked saddened by something. Something had upset her.

'What's the matter Eileen? Not bad news I hope,'

'No, not exactly. Just unexpected news.'
'What was it, the news, then?'
'You won't really want to hear it, I daresay.'
'I won't know at all unless you tell me. Come on my girl, out with it.'
'It was only Richard, wishing us all the best and so on. He says that he might call over, mid- November probably. He has news for us; something he's seen in the Church Times and he said he'd rather tell us face to face.'

And then they were both quiet for a moment and Hubert just replied, 'I see,' but as he looked at Eileen there was a darkness to his countenance. He found himself wondering about the telephone call and what exactly had been said between Eileen and her brother during the conversation, and what, if anything, Eileen had omitted to tell him.

Hubert's underlying suspicion was that his wife hadn't told him the whole story. He also felt it best that he say nothing more, so that was where he left things and nothing more was said, but for him, the day had been soured.

November 1928

Jack France was sitting in the library at Manordale. He was relaxing by the fire and enjoying a fine single malt. He was also briefly lost in his thoughts and the crackle of the fire in the grate was strangely satisfying, almost soporific. Such were the thoughts that occupied him he had almost forgotten that Graves was also in the room, awaiting Jack's further instruction.

Arthur Graves had remained standing by the door, waiting for Jack to say something further; he did not. At what he considered to be a suitable elapse of time, Graves decided to break the silence; to try and gain Mr France's attention. Graves coughed, lightly. There was no response from Mr France. Graves then wondered whether Mr France had heard this attempt, but let it go by, in any case. After a few more minutes Graves decided to speak, 'Pardon Sir, will there be anything else?'

Jack turned to face Graves in a kind of stupor. It seemed an age to Graves before Mr France responded but eventually he did. 'Sorry Arthur. I apologise. I was miles   away,   along   with   my   thoughts.'

There was another short pause and then Jack

France resumed where he had left off.

'All in all it hasn't been a bad old year has it?'

'No sir, it's not been a bad year at all.'

'That's what I thought. And Lily, Lily and Mrs Hindmarsh, I suppose they're getting on with all the preparation for the Christmas Ball? And Mrs Whittaker, she'll no doubt be giving out sound advice on what should and shouldn't be done?'

'Yes sir. The ladies have taken everything in their stride. And young Emily, she's proving to be an asset, or so Lily tells me. So, it's all in hand. And the date is settled, you don't want anything to change. I take it the ball will be the same date as it usually is, December 23rd? That's what we're all working to, anyway.'

'Of course the date stays. That was always as it was in my Father's day, part of the Manordale tradition and some things just don't change, do they?'

'No sir. Traditions here are set in stone.' Graves replied.

'Well now, that will be all, Arthur. I'll ring down later for a supper tray to be brought up.' Jack glanced at his wristwatch. 'It's just coming up to eight o' clock. I'll ring down about nine; just a sandwich and a pot of tea will be sufficient.'

'And the sandwich, sir, what would you require?'

'Something simple.' There was a pause while Jack deliberated and finally, ' I know, I shall have two rounds of cheese on toast, with a splash of Lea and Perrins. And please, tell Lily that I apologise for this. I know that by nine o'clock Mrs Hindmarsh will have left for home. And at this time of the year the days at Manordale always seem to be endless affairs with so much to do and organise. And, do you know, I'm thankful for the staff I have here at Manordale. Nothing would run as smoothly as it does without you all here.'

'I'll let Lily and Mrs Hindmarsh know. But we all know that we're appreciated. That's what makes it such a pleasant place to work. And of course, I'll also mention your supper to Lily. Thank you, sir.'

'Thank you, Graves.'

When Arthur returned to the kitchen Lily was talking with Mrs Hindmarsh who was just getting into her coat in preparation for going home. 'Everything all right, Arthur?' Lily asked, 'You look quite concerned.' Arthur began to speak and both Lily and Mrs Hindmarsh turned to face him. 'It's Mr France. He seems a little distant this evening as though there was something bothering him. In fact, at one point I wondered if he was ill or something; it was as if he was in a different world, and when he spoke it was odd when he set off, he began by saying that it hadn't been a bad old year and so on but then he went on to ask about the plans for the Christmas Ball and he was back to his old self again. I told him everything was in hand and he seemed as though everything *was* all right. But I've known Mr France for such a long time; I know he's thinking about something. And there was a letter on the chair to the side of him. It was opened, so I am assuming he had read it, perhaps before I went into the library. And that's all. Something's bothering him or I'm making things up. Oh, and he also said he was grateful for the staff he has here. He appreciates how we all keep things running smoothly for him. That aside, Lily, he has asked for two rounds of cheese on toast and a pot of tea at about nine o' clock. He'll ring down. Oh, and he wants me to apologise to you as he knows Mrs Hindmarsh will have left by then.' Mrs Hindmarsh piped up, 'Shall I stay, Lily, and get everything prepared before I go? You'll only have to put it under the grill then. It won't take you so long. And you've been on your feet nearly all day, what with the preparations and planning for the Christmas Ball and who is staying over and making sure the rooms are prepared.' Lily smiled. 'It's kind of you Mrs Hindmarsh, but I'll manage with two slices of cheese on toast. Now you get off home. I know you've worked flat out today, so thank you. And would you like Arthur to escort you. It's dark out there, and I wouldn't relish the thought of walking, not at night. Even just five minutes seems an age when you're on your own.'

'Honestly Lily, you've no need to worry over me. I'll be fine; and I've my trusty torch with me.' Mrs Hindmarsh held her torch aloft to demonstrate its versatility. 'It's a light and a weapon, if needs be,' she said. Lily laughed. 'All right Mrs Hindmarsh, and I hope you never need to use it as a weapon.'

When Mrs Hindmarsh had left Lily sat down at the kitchen table with Arthur. ' I wonder what news the letter held that has had such an effect on Mr France,' she said. Arthur remained silent and merely shrugged his shoulders but he thought everything about his and Mr France's earlier conversation 'odd'.

A few minutes after nine o'clock, the bell in the library rang. Arthur knew what it would be and he waited for Lily to get everything together on a tray so that he could take it up to Mr France. A little before ten past nine Arthur began his short journey. He tapped at the library door and Mr France bade him enter. Arthur quickly scanned the room as he walked across to the table that was in the bay of the library window and where he placed the supper tray. The curtains were open, which was unusual; as it was winter it was a common practice that most of the curtains at Manordale were drawn by four in the afternoon. 'Thank you, Arthur,' Jack said as Arthur turned to walk towards the library door. There was a brief pause of no more than three seconds and again Jack spoke. He had in his hand an envelope. He waved it back and forth and then spoke again, 'Arthur, before you go I have something that I have to say. It's in regard to this letter. Please sit down for a moment.' Arthur did as he was asked. 'I don't really know where to start. This letter arrived in the post this morning when I was out. I have read and re-read it at length since my return.' Arthur remained silent. He didn't quite know exactly what was expected of him. Jack must have noticed the puzzled look that was spreading across Arthur's face, for almost as suddenly as Arthur had processed his thoughts, Jack said, 'Don't look so worried, Arthur. It's nothing terrible. In fact I'm not quite sure why I'm burdening you with this at all. Do you by any chance remember my father's friend, the late Gerald Packham?'

'Can't say as I do, sir,' came the reply.

'No? Well no matter, I didn't quite think that you should but I've received this letter from his daughter, Miss Susan Packham. I must admit I have no knowledge or recollection about them at all as I don't remember the last time I met them, which I no doubt would have done but Gerald Packham has been dead for a long time, some years before my father, I believe, but it's set me in a predicament of sorts, at any rate. I perhaps had some dealings with her when I was a child, you know, visits and suchlike as you do when your parents feel obliged to take you with them wherever they happen to be going but I must say they were perhaps such very dull or uneventful events because none of them seem to have stuck in my mind. Anyway, long story short, after living in Paris for most of her adult life she is returning to live in London. Her apartment in Mayfair won't be ready until late January and she'd rather like somewhere to stay and so it looks like it will be here. That's the gist of the letter, at any rate. And honestly, how can I refuse? I'm just thinking of all the work that's connected with a Manordale Christmas, the big day itself and then the Christmas Ball and so on, and one more guest will mean another room to prepare and menus will need to be added to. Well, what do you think Arthur?'

'Not a lot to think, sir. She's bound to be coming anyway, I suppose. And do you think you could really say 'No'? It wouldn't be like you to do that, and once they're here, your memory might be jogged and you'll have a lot to catch up on. It could be rather pleasant, but only once you give the say so. Which it sounds as though you are obliged to do. We might as well make the most of it. And as I say, it could be a pleasant surprise, not the dreaded unexpected visitor as you are thinking. And Lily and Mrs Hindmarsh will cope admirably. There's always more food than enough at Manordale any day of the week so a few days over Christmas will be child's play for the ladies.'

Jack France smiled. 'I'm pleased you view it that way, Arthur. I feel a lot more at ease with the predicament now and also more up to eating my supper.' Jack stood up from the chair and walked over to the table and the supper tray. 'Tell Lily everything was admirable, Arthur. Goodnight.'

Arthur turned and left the room. He wondered sometimes at Mr France. An educated, worldly man and yet sometimes he seemed to allow the tiniest of things play on his mind.

December 16th 1928

'What are you up to today, Lily?' Arthur asked his wife as they both readied themselves to leave their estate cottage and start their short walk across to Manordale.

Lily fastened the pin into her hat and picked up her gloves as she spoke, 'I expect the trees will be delivered at some point, the big one for the entrance hall, after that's in place I suppose Mrs Hindmarsh and Mrs Whittaker will be entrusted with the decoration, once the tree is secure. It's always a worry to me, these big trees in the hall, even the smaller ones are large in comparison to ours at the cottage. I'm afraid they'll topple or something will set them alight, well anyway, you know me and that's just the way I am. I know the hall will look beautiful when all the trees are in place, but I wouldn't swap our little tree for any of the ones in the hall. And there's less to worry about as well.' And then Lily took Arthur's hand, and smiled before she continued, 'And the decoration alone usually takes the best part of two days, as you should be aware, Arthur. For me, I will be in my room trying to put menus together with Mrs Hindmarsh as a guide, of course, for the 22nd, when the guests begin to arrive. And there's still no word of Mr France's distant friend, Miss Packham. I find it very odd myself, that a distant friend should just turn up, well invite themselves, really. Even if their Mayfair apartment is being redecorated . . .'

'Lily, it's nothing to do with you, not that, anyway. That's all for Mr France to decide upon. Now, come on and we can talk on the way across to the house. And a childhood family friend isn't that distant. Not in the scheme of things.'

'Not if you see them more than once in a blue moon, no,' Lily replied. Arthur tugged at her hand, he knew his wife and her ideas and sometimes when she had the bit between her teeth there was nothing that could be done. Things just had to run their course with her. It's the way she was. Arthur tried to change the way of the conversation, but nothing could persuade Lily to stop.   Arthur just nodded and hmmed, at what he thought   were   the   appropriate   moments.

There wasn't long left until Christmas and they would be busy at the hall, Arthur knew that but perhaps a short London trip and a visit to Oxford street and one of the stores? That might well be something he might suggest. It could perhaps be something that Lily might look forward to. Swan and Edgar sprang to mind; and it had the all-important restaurant. Arthur decided not to mention it just yet. In case he couldn't pull it off. There was nothing worse than the let-down of a good idea that goes awry.

The minutes passed and they soon arrived at Manordale and for most of this time they were silent. Arthur not wanting to mention his London idea just yet. Then Lily turned suddenly and smiled and said, 'Arthur, you never mentioned what you would be up to today.'

'That's because I'm not really sure. Mr France wants me to meet him at the stables. I can't for one moment think what's going to happen.'

The hall was always a hive of activity this close to Christmas. Tradition was something that eked out of the very fabric of Manordale and something that Jack found he revelled in, even though any new-fangled gadget soon found its way into Manordale; Jack was definitely interested in anything new that came out and he would give most things a try. Jack felt this was important and the right thing to do; to move forward while carrying the past along at the same time.

One tradition that was started by Jack's parents was the masked costume ball and Jack was more than pleased to carry things on. Whatever day of the week it fell, the masked ball was always on the 23rd of December and it was an opportunity for the France family to host the gathering for their staff as well as anyone from Moretondale who wanted to attend.

The masked ball Jack would be hosting this year would follow along exactly the same lines as those started by his parents when they first came to Manordale over forty years ago. All the staff worked hard throughout the year and extra work was placed upon them in the run up to Christmas, so the 23rd was when the staff could enjoy being hosted by the France family and outside staff were brought in to help with the occasion. To serve those who served.

There was also a party funded by Mr France for the schoolchildren who attended the local village school. There was plenty of food, which the teachers helped to organise, there were party games and each child received a small gift. Mr France had in mind that a visit from Father Christmas might happen this year. The trap, out in the stable and not used for years, could be decked out as though it were a sleigh and be pulled from the hall to the school. It would be driven of course by Father Christmas himself and pulled by a sufficiently obliging pony. Jack just needed to find one. The Manordale estate no longer had ponies and the tenant farmers had larger horses if they had anything at all. Jack had envisaged the whole thing in his mind. It would be a spectacle for the children to behold. Something they would always remember.

Jack was hopeful that Grainger would be able to give him some assistance with this idea in order to pull the whole thing off.

The Christmas trees for the hall were due to be delivered at eleven o'clock. The trees at Manordale were always ordered from Mr Booth's Forestry and Tree Felling. The largest tree, the one for the entrance hall, was about eight to ten feet in height and they were always ordered to have quite a good 'skirt' with plenty of spaces, so that the decorations could hang between boughs.

At three minutes past eleven the trees arrived. Lily had to admit, even with all the extra work that went with this time of year, that she loved it. A fresh pine fragrance wafted throughout the hall. It was that wonderful feeling of the outside being brought in. She came through to supervise as the largest of the trees was put in place. Everything had been measured to make sure the tree was a snug fit. It was then held secure by wooden pegs that wedged it into place. When Lily stood back to take a look at it, she had to admit that it looked perfectly well, even without any decorations.

The next tree to find its place was a smaller one of about five to six feet tall and that was put into the dining room and after that a five foot one was manoeuvred into position in the drawing room. That done, it was time to offer the men a glass of sherry. Mrs Hindmarsh then did the honours with hot mince pies fresh from the oven. She too, loved this time of year and the way that Christmas made everyone seem happy with their lot, whatever it might be.

When the men had departed Lily said, 'Well, Mrs Hindmarsh, what do you think?' Mrs Hindmarsh took one look at the large tree and said, 'It's grand,' and then with a smile added, I'll get young Frank to bring in the decorations. This one will take some dressing!'

Mrs Whittaker arrived just before two o'clock and when she had removed her coat and prepared herself for work, she set to her business for the afternoon. First, she would clear up any mess left by the 'tree men' and then she would polish the 'main items' of furniture with wax furniture polish until they gleamed. The warmth from the fires that had been lit in various of the Manordale rooms made the scents of polish and pine mingle. There was no other time of year quite like this.

All of this work took about an hour and as the clock in the hall chimed the half hour, Mrs Hindmarsh came up from the kitchen to call Mrs Whittaker down for tea and mince pies. This was the moment everyone looked forward to and Mrs Whittaker was quick to leave her chores behind her and join with the others in the kitchen.

In the kitchen, young Terry Franks was busy opening boxes of Christmas baubles that had been wrapped and carefully put away earlier in the year. Emily, who hadn't seemed to have much time for the young man, had, since her birthday a few months earlier taken quite a shine to him. Mrs Hindmarsh and Lily quietly smiled to each other as the pair chatted easily with one another while sorting through the tree decorations.

While all this activity was taking place in the house, Jack was down at the garage speaking with Grainger. He would also soon need to have a chat with Arthur if his Christmas plan was to come off.

Grainger suggested that Mr France might try Vale Court and the Dennistoun Hardie stable in his search for a pony to pull the Christmas sled. 'I had considered that,' Jack said, 'but Lord Hardie has only the stud stallions, now, or so I believe.'

'Well,' Grainger replied, 'I have it on good authority from Fred that Lord Dennistoun Hardie has acquired a young filly that could be just what you're looking for. A nice young thing and a good temperament. She's not too tall so the children wouldn't be alarmed by her and she's placid, which I suppose is what you'd be looking for.'

'Have you seen her, then?' Jack asked.

'Of course I have. Fred's a friend and we go for a drink together, so news gets spread around. Apparently, Lord Dennistoun Hardie had been thinking of acquiring a mare for a good few months and when Tess came up for sale, he sent Fred over to have a look, the report was good and so the next time they went over was to strike the deal. Fred accompanied Lord Dennistoun Hardie and the deal was done then and there.'

'Where did he get her from, do you know?'

'Batchelor's stud on the Wycombe Road. She's lovely looking as well, as horses go. Chestnut with a white flash.'

Jack smiled. 'I hope Dennistoun Hardie doesn't have any plans for the festive season himself where she's needed; it could scupper my plans. I'll go back to the house and telephone him now and arrange to go over in the morning. Thanks for your help Grainger. And while I'm here, there was one more thing. The old trap that belonged to my mother, I thought that it would come in as a faux sleigh, as it were. The gifts for the children in sacks by the side of Arthur, who I hope will dress as Father Christmas for the occasion.' Grainger stifled a laugh as he replied to Mr France; the thought of Arthur as Father Christmas!

'No trouble Mr France. I'll go over to the old stable block and see if I can get the trap of your mother's and give it a clean-up. As I recall it's been against the back wall gathering dust.'

'I would imagine so. Anyway, you're on to it and that's good. We haven't got much time really to get organised, what with the guests arriving over the next few days and I'd like to get ahead a little if I can with everything I have planned'. Jack turned slightly, and as he did he paused and turned back to face Grainger, 'And Grainger, not a word to Arthur until I have all the relevant plans in place, as it were. I wouldn't want to scare him off.'

Grainger took a cigarette from his waistcoat pocket and lit it. He threw the match out onto the cobbles and watched momentarily as Mr France walked the path from the old stables and across towards Manordale.

Grainger smoked his cigarette, savouring every moment. When he had finished smoking Grainger went back inside the garage and squeezed the lit end of the cigarette between his fingers to make sure it was fully extinguished. He then went through the door at the back of the garage and across the stable yard and opened the stable door. It creaked. It was dark and Grainger went back to the garage for a torch. He mumbled as he went back into the stable, 'Where does he get these ideas from?' and he was shaking his head as he said the words quietly to himself; and then he proceeded to drag out the trap from what had been its place of rest for most of the previous ten years.

December 17th

Jack walked directly round to the stables once he had arrived at Vale Court. Fred was waiting for him and met him in the yard. 'I hear you'd like to see our Tess, Mr France.'

'Yes. Has Lord Dennistoun Hardie had a word with you?'

'He has. Follow me, she's over here. We've had a new stable built just for her. She's pretty special, we think.'

The two men walked across the yard and just off to the left was a brand-new stable block. Jack admired it and then he followed Fred inside. The stable smelt of new wood and hay and horse.

'Here she is, sir, in number two.' The young filly obviously had got used to Fred and whinnied softly when she saw him. 'You can get close to her, she's neither nervous nor too much to handle. She's just about right,' Fred said.

Jack approached Tess and patted her muzzle; she moved her head around Jack's hand and gently nuzzled him.

There were footsteps heard as Lord Dennistoun Hardie came into the stable. 'I see you're getting acquainted with young Tess, Jack.'

'I am. She's a lovely, young filly. I think you've bought a gem, if you don't mind me saying.'

'Not at all, Jack.'

Plans were hastily made and Lord Dennistoun Hardie said that perhaps they should carry on with their conversation inside the house, it would be warmer; and no more than a few minutes later Jack and Lord Dennistoun Hardie were making their way from the stables and into the warmth of Vale Court. Once inside, the two men were soon settled in the lounge and there was whisky already poured and waiting for them on a small table by the window alcove.

'Take your whisky, Jack, any will do. I asked Pennyquick to pour it and let it breathe so it would be good for us, directly before I left for the stables. It should be at its best now, let's not wait any longer.'

Whisky in hand the two men moved closer to the fire. It was a dark morning and seemed as though that was how it would stay for the rest of the day.

'And you're certain she'll do for what you have in mind, Jack?'

'I would say she's ideal. Thank you for offering her to me. I thought it would be exciting for the children to have Father Christmas himself deliver their gifts to the school after the party. It's the day after tomorrow, the 19th, and then they finish for the Christmas holidays. I can remember how it made me feel the final week of school. Mind you, I was a boarder for a time at King's School, Canterbury. A good school but I was always pleased when it was the holidays. Any holidays. I just wanted to come home. To be set free from the confines of the school routine did my heart a power of good.'

'I remember that your father mentioned something of the sort, but once the war had started he thought you would be safer there, for the duration.'

'I did manage to get home early though. 1917. That was a huge relief. I think both to the staff and to me. A good school. I just wasn't the overly academic type, I suppose.'

Lord Dennistoun Hardie smiled. 'Not all of us are, academic. Our talents lie in other directions, that's what makes life so interesting, you never know where it will take you. Now, to get back to the task in hand. Will you be bringing the trap here on the 19th?'

'I think that's best. If the trap's in a suitable condition when I get back to Manordale I'll perhaps call round with it tomorrow. We could have a trial run.'

'I shan't be here tomorrow. Going off to London, business, but just go round to the stable. Fred will get everything ready.'

Jack drank the last of the whisky from the tumbler and stood up, returning the glass to the table. 'That was appreciated, as is the offer of Tess. I'll get off now and see what the progress is with the trap. I've left Grainger getting it all ready. So, we'll leave it at that and then we'll see Fred tomorrow, ten-thirty -ish?'

'I'm sure that will be all right. I'll let Fred know.'

When he arrived back at Manordale, Jack went straight round to the garage to see Grainger. He had worked wonders with the trap and Jack was more than pleased.

'I've arranged for us to go across to Vale Court tomorrow for a trial run with Tess. The party's on the 19th before the children break for school, so I hope this all turns out well. Is ten-thirty in the morning all right with you?' Jack asked.

'Shouldn't be a problem,' Grainger replied.

Jack left and walked across to the house. As soon as the door was opened the scent of pine and cinnamon filled the air. Jack never tired of this season. It was, he believed, a season of hope. His quiet reverie was broken by Lily who walked into the hall as he entered. 'Oh, Mr France, I'm so relieved to see you. It's been so hectic since you left.'

'I'll just attend to one or two things in my study and then I'll come down to your rooms, and by the way, is Arthur anywhere close at hand?'

'That's part of the 'hectic',' Lily said, 'shall I carry on or tell all in a few minutes.'

'I'd rather like a few minutes,' Jack replied, 'I've a couple of things to make a note of but I shan't be long.'

'Thank you, sir,' Lily replied.

True to his word Jack France arrived at Lily's door no more than fifteen minutes after their meeting in the hall. 'Mr France, please sit down, there's quite a lot to get through.' Jack noted the anxious look on Lily's face and tried to put her at her ease. 'I think *you* should sit down Lily and try and relax. You look all in.'

Lily somewhat unceremoniously flopped into her armchair and made herself comfortable on the cushions. 'I'll start with Arthur first, seeing as you asked about him.'

'Very well,' Jack replied.

'He's had an accident, a minor one but he's broken his leg, it seems. He's at the hospital now. They're setting it. But what a time to happen, just over a week to Christmas and he's got a broken leg. He'll be no more help with all the things we have to prepare. I'm so sorry Mr France.'

'Don't you worry yourself, Lily. As long as he's all right, that is the main thing. I know breaks take a while to heal; sometimes as much as eight weeks to set properly but he has as long as it takes. Please let him know that won't you?'

'I think he does know. You are always so good to us, well to all the staff, and we thank you for that.'

'Well, as long as he's all right. When will he be ready to come back home? Grainger could fetch him.'

'The hospital will telephone when he's ready to be discharged. If it gets too late into the day, it will be tomorrow, in the morning.'

'We'll manage it somehow,' Jack replied. There was a slight look of consternation on Jack's face. He had suddenly realised that Arthur was not going to be available for the role of Father Christmas. Lily studied Jack's face and when he didn't say anything more she asked, 'Shall I carry on, sir?'

'Oh, I suppose you should, Lily.'

'Your post is here,' she said as she passed the letter tray with several letters on it across to Mr France, who took the letters from it and then put them into his jacket pocket. 'Arthur took them from the postman this morning. The post office seems to be getting out extra deliveries, it being so close to the big day. It was one of his final duties, shall we say, before he tripped.'

'Tripped? How exactly did it happen, was he in the house or outside?'

'I suppose you could say he was outside. He was just stepping from the hall to the porch, and he went.

That was it. I don't think he really knows what happened.'

'How did he get to the hospital? The only ambulance that the cottage hospital has available is the horse drawn one and it's difficult to get hold of at times.'

'Luckily, Dr. Blaikie called in to see you, which is really where I should have started my tale. He wanted to let you know that he will be going up to Scotland staying with family so, he won't be able to attend the Christmas Ball but he said to let you know that once he gets settled in the village he looks forward to many years of Christmas events in Moretondale. Anyway, Arthur had just been incapacitated when Dr Blaikie called, and with Dr. Blaikie having a car, he kindly immobilised Arthur's leg and, I don't know how, but he manoeuvred Arthur into his car and then he drove Arthur down to the cottage hospital.'

'Good job he appeared. And it will also be good for Moretondale to have its own doctor. The twentieth century is certainly a good time to be alive. And here, in good old Britannia we've a lot to be thankful for. Was there anything else, Lily?'

'Yes, just one more thing. Your old friend Miss Packham has telephoned. She will be arriving sometime after one o'clock on the 19th. And she will be accompanied by her companion, Miss Waterstone. So, it looks like Mrs Whittaker will have to prepare another two rooms. I haven't spoken to her yet, and I could always ask Emily. Mrs Whittaker, as you know can likely get a bit tetchy, particularly if she thinks she's being overworked.'

'You are quite understanding, Lily, of everyone, I might add. Thank you. And I would give the extra work over to Emily. Miss Susan Packham can have the red room on the second floor, and the room opposite will suffice for her companion.'

Lily made a note of the arrangements in her housekeeping diary which over the last few days had suddenly had more entries added that were in need of her attention. It wasn't a problem to Lily. A natural organiser, she had always relished a challenge.

'Right Lily. If you think that's all, I'll go and attend to these letters,' and Jack tapped his jacket pocket before adding, 'and I have a few telephone calls to make. Oh, and Albert Riggs, is he still out and about? I haven't seen him in the village of late.'

'Arthur caught him in the *Ring o'Bells* the night before last. He's hale and hearty.'

'Splendid. I'll go over to have a word with him this afternoon. He could be just the man I need.'

Jack left Lily to her work and went into his study and put his letters on the desk. A few were Christmas cards and he separated all the post into piles. In one pile the cards, in another, letters from those whose handwriting he recognised, and in another, those whose handwriting he didn't recognise, and in yet another those that had the whiff of 'official' about them.

The cards he opened and placed on the library mantel. There were none from forgotten friends or relatives. The letters in both piles were insignificant and Jack put those in his desk drawer. *Now for the official ones*, he thought. Of the three letters, one was from the local golf club inviting Jack to the new year bash. Jack was not a member of the club and would not be attending. He would reply to that later. The second was advertising, bumfodder, for the bin. The third was from the diocese. The church in Moretondale hadn't had an incumbent for nearly two years. Perhaps this would be informing Jack, as Patron of the church that a new vicar was on the cards. He opened the letter and read it through carefully. It was as he thought. A new vicar, Reverend Richard Smythe, would be arriving in January. He hoped to call in and visit with Jack on the 23rd, before taking up the reins completely in January. It also mentioned that although he would have liked to stay and hopefully lead a short carol service at St. Stephen's on Christmas Eve, he was unfortunately otherwise engaged.

Jack left the letter opened out on his desk. Suddenly the festive season was becoming very busy indeed.

Jack could see the day ahead, or what was left of it, would be hectic. If he was to get everything done he would have to get to it. He telephoned Hamley's and placed an order for assorted toys for boys and girls, average age, eight years. He was assured they should be delivered by their own transport the following day. That done, he walked across to see Maggie Evans at the shop. She usually had a good supply of chocolate novelties at this time of year. 'Good morning, Mr France,' she said as he walked through the door.

'Good Morning, Maggie. It's very festive in here, what with all the decorations,' he replied as he glanced around Maggie's shop.

'I like to make an effort,' she said, smiling.

'Well you know what I've come in for. Chocolate for the school children. An Assortment. Enough for twenty-five, make that thirty, children. Better to have too much than not enough.'

Maggie set to work getting all the required chocolate into a bag, chatting away as she did. 'I notice the manse has been boarded up. Reckon that'll go up for sale in the new year after all the shenanigans that went on, and getting Albert Riggs involved as well, shameful. And then there's St. Stephen's, I hear a new Reverend will be there come the new year, though I 'spect you'll have heard already, being a patron and so on, and will there be a carol service I wonder? He might just pop in and do something short for us if he's time, of course. I've missed the church services, I have. It's better in the church, the atmosphere and so on. I reckon that's what's been missing these last months, the church services, it's not the same in the village hall. It was all right to a point and I know we had to try and make do, but we didn't seem to get many emeritus clergy who could visit on a regular basis, and so we weren't always in the church. That was the part that dismayed me most. Not being regular in church. Although I 'spose it should be, but, no, it's not the same without a preacher, I don't care what anybody says, and how's Arthur Graves, with his leg, sounds nasty if you ask me . . .'

        Maggie Evans said all this without pausing for breath. Jack had no time to answer anything as he paid for his order and tipped his hat to Maggie before he left the shop. He did however wonder where Maggie got her news from, and how it managed to be so accurate.

        Jack returned to Manordale and was looking forward to lunch. He knew that Miss Susan Packham was arriving on the 19th with her companion, Miss Waterstone and that he wasn't quite sure what to expect. He also had the little matter of persuading Albert Riggs to be Father Christmas for the day. He would go and see him directly after lunch and hope to find him at home.

At 2.30p.m. Jack set off on the short walk to Albert Riggs' cottage. He would be there before three o'clock. The afternoon was chill but thankfully there was no sign of snow yet.

Albert Riggs opened the door of his cottage. 'Mr France, come in sir, please do.'

'I'm not disturbing your afternoon, I hope.'

'Far from it. I always enjoy having a visitor. Come in and make yourself at home.'

There was a fire roaring away in the grate and the room was delightfully smoky. Jack thought that if he sat too long with Albert in the warmth and dim light of the cottage he would soon fall asleep.

'Would you like a drop of whisky, sir. I have a new bottle in the cupboard.'

'Only if you're having one, Albert. Don't go to any trouble.'

Albert took two glasses and the bottle from the cupboard. 'It looks like you've twisted my arm sir,' he said.

The two men settled in their chairs by the fire. 'I feel slightly awkward about this, Albert, but I've come across to ask a favour of you. It's Father Christmas. I'd thought that this year Father Christmas might visit the children at the school and bring them their gifts. I'll supply everything you need. I must tell you now that I was going to ask Arthur to be 'it' but . . .' Albert interrupted, 'But he's got a broken leg,' he said.

'Yes, he has,' Jack replied.

'I'd be delighted to oblige,' Albert said, 'I used to do it in your father's time. My costume is in the loft. I haven't changed much. It still should fit. And it's the 19th, isn't it, for the schoolchildren?'

'Yes. After they've had lunch. About 1.30p.m. I've written all the details on here,' and Jack handed Albert a piece of paper.

Jack was quiet and he pondered for a moment and then looked straight at Albert. 'I see. So, it was you at Manordale when I was a boy?'

'Who else, sir?' Albert replied.

December 18th

Jack decided that this was the morning that he had for all the Christmas activities that were in some way connected to Manordale.

He breakfasted early and then went in to check with Lily and Mrs Hindmarsh regarding the plans for the ball and how they were coming along. As expected, Lily had everything under control regarding the house in general and Mrs Hindmarsh and her menu planning, in most part to accommodate the guests who were expected at Manordale, was as Mrs Hindmarsh said, *'simmering along nicely'*. Emily was helping wherever she could and Mrs Hindmarsh offered praise for the young girl, '*an asset to Manordale*,' she said. And Emily was herself, enjoying every moment of the forthcoming Christmas season at Manordale.

Jack suggested that when the order from Hamley's arrived that Mrs Whittaker should be drafted in to wrap the gifts. 'That's something she'll enjoy doing,' Lily said. Jack smiled. He asked after Terry Franks and it was no surprise to him when Lily said, 'Wherever Grainger and the cars are, that's where you'll find Terry.'

Terry Franks helped around the estate when he was needed but he was now spending a lot of time at the garage with Grainger. Terry Franks fancied that chauffeur to Mr France would be something he could aspire to, perhaps in a few years' time.

After a few minutes catching up on everything Jack said, 'Right, I'm going over to Vale Court but first I have to call in on Grainger and see how he's getting on with the trap. I also want to have a word with Riley on the way out. It's time the lights were up and lit on the large pine on the drive. It's our 'welcoming' tree. It must be lit.'

'I've spoken with Riley earlier,' Lily said, 'and he should be getting on with that now.'

'Oh, I almost forgot, Lily, how's Arthur,?' Jack asked.

'It was decided that he should be kept in the hospital overnight. It was too late for him to come home yesterday so I'm expecting him to be back home for teatime. Fingers crossed.'

'If there's anything you need Lily, just ask. I must get off to Vale Court now, so I shall see you all later.'

Jack was pleased to see that Grainger had made a first-class job with the trap. There was also a rug on the polished leather seat, should it be needed. And there were bright red sacks there, too; just right for the toys they were to hold tomorrow.

Also, as Lily had suggested, Terry Franks was at the garage with Grainger and he accepted the offer of going over to Vale Court and helping Grainger with the trap. Jack left Grainger and Franks to get organised and arranged to meet them at the front of the house in half an hour. He was now going to speak with Riley.

As he walked down the drive Jack could see Riley leaning ladders against the pine tree. There was a box on the ground. 'Good morning, Riley. All organised, I see. Do you need any help with the lights.

It probably is a two-man job. And Arthur isn't here today.'

'It's all right Mr France. Once I get all the top lights looped into the branches it's just a matter of walking around the tree. To let the tree work for you. A couple of hours should see it done.'

'That's all right then. I'll get back up to the house. Young Franks and Grainger should be waiting for me. If anyone asks for me, I'm at Vale Court. I'll be back around noon.'

'As you say, sir.'

When Jack, Grainger and Franks arrived at Vale Court, Fred and Lord Dennistoun Hardie were already at the stables waiting for them.

Lord Dennistoun Hardie spoke as the three men arrived. Grainger and Terry Franks had walked the trap to Vale Court under Jack's supervision. Once near the stable, they released their grip on the trap and let it stand on the cobbles. The wheels were wedged so that the trap wouldn't move when they tried Tess in harness.

'I must say, Grainger, you've worked hard to get the trap ready in time for tomorrow. I know from Jack that it has spent the last few years at the back of the old stable block at Manordale,' Lord Dennistoun Hardie said, 'but good work on your part. It looks splendid.'

'It was a pleasure for me to work on it and to see it have some use again,' Grainger replied.

'Jack, you come with me and you can have a look at Tess. She's ready to go,' Lord Dennistoun Hardie said. The two men walked into the stable. 'Well Jack, what do you think?'

'I think she's just the job. And I've arranged for Albert Riggs to be Father Christmas at the school. I don't know if you heard about Arthur Graves? He's broken his leg.'

'So, you're a man down and at a busy time of year for Manordale. Are you ready for the big event?' 'It's a tradition I don't want to lose,' Jack replied.

'Lady Dennistoun Hardie is very partial to the masked ball on the 23rd. In fact we're both looking forward to it.'

Lord Dennistoun Hardie called for Fred, and Grainger and Terry Franks followed on behind the two men. 'You can harness Tess to the trap, now,' Lord Dennistoun Hardie said, and he and Jack came back out into the fresh air. A few moments later Fred led Tess and the trap into the stable yard.

Jack studied the horse and trap for a few moments. 'The children will be very excited tomorrow. I am sure of it. Would it be an imposition if we left the trap here? Grainger and young Franks will come along tomorrow and lend a hand, and Albert Riggs has all the details, so, he'll arrive here in plenty of time to be ready to go across to the school and as soon as I can I'll come across and bring the sacks of gifts for the children. Then I'm afraid I'm going to be rather busy for an hour as I have guests arriving but I'm hoping to be back at the school to speak to the staff and children before they break up for the holiday. And of course, I have chocolate to distribute.'

'Do whatever makes it easier for you, Jack. Oh, and by the way, are you prepared for all the work as host on the 23rd? It's always a difficult and very hands on job. I don't think I'd like to host such a large event for the village.'

'I'm working on it, and you do get used to it, you know,' Jack replied, adding, 'the masks, as was my parents' idea, are all under the portico before you enter the house. Just take one from the box and put it on before you come inside; and as usual, no removing cloaks before you're in the house. No one must see the costumes before you're all masked up!'

Lady Dennistoun Hardie appeared in the stable yard. 'I thought I must come and see how you were all getting on. I've been a little busy today, trying on my outfit for the masked ball,' and she paused as she pushed a finger to her lips and whispered, 'but I'm not giving anything away.'

There were smiles as Lady Dennistoun Hardie spoke. She then went over to Tess and made a fuss of her, 'She's beautiful, I hope you all agree,' she said, and then she took a sugar lump from her jacket pocket and held out her hand to Tess, who took the sweet treat, willingly.

Jack, Grainger, and Franks left Vale Court. 'I just need to go and check with Albert that all's set with him for tomorrow. I'll see you both back at Manordale within the hour. My meeting with Albert shouldn't take long.' And with that, Jack France took the road to Albert Riggs' cottage.

Albert Riggs was in; the door was slightly open and as Jack called out, Albert replied with, 'I'm in the parlour Mr France, come on through.'

Jack found Albert by the fire. The room was hot and Jack found it rather stifling but it seemed to suit Albert. 'Sit down then, Mr France. You know we don't stand on ceremony here.'

Once seated Jack asked if Albert was still in agreement to be Father Christmas and he said he was and that he'd tried on his costume and the suit still fitted him, as he knew it would.

'That's good. And you have all the details I passed on to you, so you're able to be across at Vale Court, tomorrow for one-ish?'

'I can do that, sir,' Albert replied, and then tapped the side of his head, 'It's all up here sir. A mental note.'

'Good. Pleased to hear it. Grainger will be at Vale Court to help get you get organised with all your packages and into the trap, should you need it. And the trap which Grainger has worked on has come up very nicely, I must say. And Tess, the filly from Vale Court is very amenable. We've just been up to Vale Court to see her. It's good of Lord Dennistoun Hardie to let us use her. Oh, and Grainger will also be bringing over to Vale Court the sacks of toys for the children. I've set Mrs Whittaker on the task of wrapping the gifts. I'm afraid that I won't be able to join you at Vale Court but I will be getting across to the school as soon as I am able. An old acquaintance of my father's, Gerald Packham, well his daughter Susan and her companion will be staying at Manordale over Christmas and into the new year while Miss Packham's apartment in Mayfair is being redecorated and they arrive at Manordale tomorrow. The thing is, I can't say that I can recall the Packham family clearly but that's childhood for you, if it isn't important to you, you don't really retain the knowledge.

Anyway, it's put me in a bit of a fix if I'm perfectly honest but these things do have to be done sometimes.'

'It can be awkward having guests who you can't remember. A bit of a tricky one that and no mistake, Mr France.'

'Yes. Anyway, I'll make it to the school as soon as I can and I shall have chocolate novelties that I will ask for your help to distribute, if you don't mind.'

'You don't know how much I'm looking forward to it Mr France. It's good to feel involved. It takes me back to your father's time at the hall. Good times.'

'I'm glad you view it that way, Albert. And are you coming to the ball. Have you got your costume ready?'

'I have, sir. And it won't be as Father Christmas,' Albert said. Both men laughed at the joke and then Jack continued, 'Before I take my leave, I have one more question for you. I've just come by the Old Manse and it's boarded up. Maggie Evans mentioned that she thought it might be coming up for sale. I don't suppose you've heard anything, Albert?'

'No. I saw the men who boarded it up, though. They were here most of the morning and they just did the ground floor as you perhaps noticed but there's been no land agent round and nothing mentioned in Leigh's in Melford. I checked their window when I was in town.

I didn't go in to ask. Thought they wouldn't take kindly to the likes of me asking about such a property.'

'You're quick off the mark there, Albert. Thanks for that news. Right, I'll be on my way and I'll just go and have a walk around the manse grounds. Make sure everything seems in order.'

'What are you thinking, sir? Do you think it's odd?'

'I'm not sure Albert. Time will tell, I suppose, and don't get up. I can see myself out and I'll see you at the school tomorrow.'

The sun was shining, putting on a brave face in a winter-grey world. And now as Jack looked at the Old Manse it looked as though it had been trapped in a world of its own. Shut off from its surroundings. The boarded-up windows and doors adding to an overall feeling of neglect, even though the property had only been left empty for a few months. Jack found himself hoping that it wouldn't be too long before someone took the property. A property shouldn't be left to go to rack and ruin, it needed new people. It needed to be cared for and not to be left empty for too long. Empty buildings were soon wont to become derelict.

Jack decided that he would speak to Leigh's land agents later, to see if the manse had been put on the books. Everything, such as it was, looked in order. The gardens were unkempt but not too overgrown. As the winter season was one of die-back and not growth there was nothing much to be done. Jack walked around the building to where the coal shed was. It was a sort of 'add on' from a previous time and was situated at the back of the property, to the right-hand side of the manse. He hadn't noticed if that had been boarded across, which made him think that it probably hadn't. As he drew closer to it, he could see it had not, and he found that strange. He pulled at the coal shed door. It didn't release easily but Jack could see there was no lock. He pulled again and this time it freed up and he managed to open the door. He looked inside. It was dark and empty and what small amount of coal there was, was piled against the back wall, towards the corner.

Jack closed the door and left everything as he had found it, he then returned to the road and continued his walk back home to Manordale. He didn't realise that he was being watched.

When Jack arrived back at Manordale there had been no more telephone calls or visitors to the house. The only arrivals had been more postal deliveries; more cards and what Jack assumed to be RSVPs for the Manordale ball.

Jack went into his study and rang down for Mrs Hindmarsh to send up some sandwiches and a pot of tea. He would lunch while he worked. He was hoping that if Miss Packham and her companion were going to arrive tomorrow that they would advise the time of their expected arrival by mid-afternoon at the latest. These things just couldn't be left to the realms of possibilities. And then there was the letter from the diocese, and the arrival of the new vicar.

Jack sat at his desk and then he re-read the letter from the diocese. Yes, it was there in black and white and he, as patron of the parish would be expected to make Reverend Smythe welcome, and then there was the carol service. The people of Moretondale were hoping that with the new vicar coming to the parish in January that he might be persuaded into leading a short carol service in the church on Christmas Eve. Jack had said that he would see what he could do. That would need some planning. He decided that he would dig out the old *nine lessons and carols* sheets that he had. If any of the previous readers were available he would draft them in. They'd done it before, they could be expected in such an emergency, to do it again.

Jack retrieved the church documents from his files and soon came across the lists. He had them all, from the first time nine lessons and carols had been held at St. Stephen's in 1920. There was a knock at the study door. It was Lily Graves. 'I've brought your sandwiches, sir.' And Lily brought the tray across to the desk where Jack was seated, 'Are you having them here or shall I put them on the corner table, sir?' 'On   the desk will be all right. I'll work around them. And Lily, pardon me for not enquiring, have you heard how Arthur is getting along?'

'No-one from the hospital has telephoned yet. I've decided to give them until 3 o'clock and then, if I may, I'll . . .' Jack interrupted, 'You don't have to ask Lily. Yes, please telephone from here.'

'Thank you, sir. Will that be all?'

'Yes and No. I want to pick your brains. It won't take long, just a couple of questions. Have you heard about the Old Manse? I suppose you know it's boarded up?'

'Yes. The thinking in the village seems to be that it will be going up for sale.'

'Yes. Maggie Evans intimated as much when I was in the shop. She also said that there'll be a new vicar at St. Stephen's in the new year. Is that what the talk about the village is?'

'Oh yes. Everybody's talking about it. I hear the new vicar, his name is Reverend Smythe or so I'm led to believe, might be here for one of the Christmas services, Christmas Eve. The boys who were in the choir before are quite excited as there will be a carol service in church again this year.'

'Thank you Lily. Now, could I just put some of those things straight? I am expecting to meet with

Reverend Smythe on the 23rd, and the facts of the carol service have yet to be decided. I have had word now from the diocese and the carol service in St. Stephen's is not on the agenda as far as they're concerned, but if the vicar cannot lead the service we'll do our own. You know we are quite a capable bunch here in Moretondale. And one more thing while I'm on the subject, I am amazed at the way news travels around this village, particularly as my letter from the diocese only arrived today.'

'Reverend Smythe has been in Maggie's shop. Maggie said that he was full of it when he called in. That's how Maggie knows. I'm sure all the village will be pleased that we've someone coming to St. Stephen's full time.'

'Reverend Smythe has been in Maggie's shop?'

'Yes. That's what Maggie told me. That's how she knew so much about what was happening with Christmas and everything.'

'Thank you for that extra information, Lily. That makes things rather more odd than I first thought. I'm hoping to meet reverend Smythe over the next day or two, the 23rd, as I said, and as I only received the letter from the diocese today informing me that the new incumbent would be here in January and of the proposed visit, it seems that my letter is already out of date. Perhaps I ought to spend more time in Maggie's to keep up to date with village events.'

Jack and Lily both laughed at the thought of Mr France's remark, but really, Jack thought it might not be a bad idea.

Jack ate his sandwiches at his desk and continued checking his lists and letters. He would check his list of readers, later. The names he had were: Mr Jack France, he decided to tick himself off. He would be available to read again. Then there was Major William Sotherby, Lord Dennistoun Hardie, Tom Carter, Sir John Percival, Mr Riley, Gerald Asquith, Albert Riggs, Terence Franks.

Jack smiled when he saw Terry Franks given his 'Sunday' name. Terry had graduated from choir to occasional reader of lessons the year his voice broke. Choirboys usually graduated to pumping the organ when this happened but Neville James' voice broke only a week or two earlier so, Terry Franks fate was sealed.

Jack ran the thoughts through in his head and wrote them down as if for clarification, though none was needed. The ball was on the 23rd, the carol service, of sorts, would take place on the 24th, and the school visit was tomorrow, the 19th, when the uninvited guests were also due to arrive, time as yet, unknown. If only there was some word.

Jack knew that those who were staying for the ball would arrive on the 22nd. He hoped none would arrive before, although it had been known on the very odd occasion, to happen. Everyone else, bar the 'extra guests' would know that it was carriages at midnight on the 23rd. But that wouldn't really matter to them.

Jack's mind went wandering again and ended up at the carol service. Would the old organist, Mr Bolton be available to play for the Christmas Eve service? He would add him to his list and make sure to get into contact with him as soon as possible.

Jack finished his lunch and left the letters on his desk. There was nothing much he could do now before he heard from Reverend Smythe or the uninvited guests. He telephoned some of the names on the list. They were all available and pleased to be invited to take part. A sense of relief passed over Jack. He pulled the bell in the study and within minutes Lily came through. 'I've finished lunch and then I shall be walking the estate, see what everyone's up to. If there are any calls for me or any visitors, get Emily to go to the garage. Grainger should be there and I will turn up there eventually. Emily can leave any messages that may come in with Grainger.'

Lily nodded and as she left the study she took the lunch tray with her.

Jack then sat for a while. He felt that not all was quite right at the Old Manse although there was nothing that seemed out of place, either. He decided to telephone Leigh's in Melford and see if they had any news. The telephone at Leigh's office rang and rang, so much so that Jack almost gave up, and when the telephone was answered it was by a young woman, who in Jack's opinion seemed rather flustered. 'Leigh's of Melford, land agents and valuers,' she said in her best telephone voice. Jack fancied that she had newly come to Melford and was trying to hide an accent.

'Hello,' she said, 'Hello, is anybody there?'

'Oh, sorry,' Jack replied, 'I was distracted for a moment, a deer just came up to the window, apologies.'

'That's quite all right, sir. Now, how can we help you today?' Her voice was calmer now and her tone more measured.

'I'm enquiring about the Old Manse on the road out to Melford. I was visiting the area earlier today and noticed it was boarded up. It made me wonder, has it come onto the market?'

'Do you mean is it for sale, sir?'

'Yes.'

'I'll check for you. Just one moment, please.'

Jack heard the sound of the telephone receiver being placed on the desk, and then the click of heels on the parquet flooring that Jack knew covered the floors of the offices of Leigh's. He then heard a filing cabinet drawer pushed heavily to closed. Then the sound of heels started and stopped again as the telephone receiver was picked up. 'Hello?' she said.

Jack replied, 'Hello, what's the news?'

'I'm sorry. I can't be of any assistance sir, but if the property is up for sale it isn't with us. I've just checked through the files.'

'Oh, sorry to have troubled you, 'bye.' And Jack replaced his telephone. That was a waste of time. He shrugged his shoulders and then he got up from his chair and put on his overcoat and set off to walk the estate.

He was able to catch up with some of the other names on the list, Riley, Franks, Asquith, and Grainger. Again there was no problem and all were keenly looking forward to the service and meeting their new vicar in due course.

There were no messages passed to Grainger from Emily.

Jack decided to check up with Albert Riggs and Tom Carter the following day.

When Jack walked back into Manordale it was almost a quarter past three. He went downstairs to Lily's room to see if there had been any news of Arthur. There had. It wasn't good. Arthur had had a bad reaction to the anaesthetic. He had required surgery to set his leg as it had required pinning, and this is where the problem had arisen. The operation however, had been a success but they needed to keep Arthur in under observation for a few more days. Lily was distraught. 'We've never spent a Christmas apart. Not since we married. Except for the war.'

'It's nearly a week to Christmas. I'm sure he'll be back home by then,' Jack said, and hoped that his remark would help to calm her worries.

Jack then returned upstairs and took a torch from the basket by the door in the hall. The light was fading fast. Jack decided to walk past the Old Manse again. He was certain something was going on; he just wasn't sure what it was.

By the time he reached the manse it was properly dark. Jack walked into the grounds and up to the house. It was impossible to see anything inside the manse as all the windows and ground floor doors were boarded over. He went round to the back of the manse. All seemed to be as it was earlier in the day. Nothing out of order. Jack crossed to the old coal shed. It was as he had left it. He retraced his steps from earlier and walked around the side of the house. All quiet, or was it? He thought he could hear someone, a man, reciting verses of the bible. He couldn't make out exactly what was being said but occasionally he heard the words, '*In the name of . . ., Amen,*' as if prayers were being said, and then, '*in the beginning*', the beginning of the first lesson in the nine lessons and carols. Jack moved on, going through the words he had heard, in his head. '*In the beginning was the word, and the word was with God and the word was God*'. John 1, Verse 1. What was going on?

Jack walked up the side of the manse, dousing his torch as he did so. If someone was in *there* he'd rather that they didn't know he was outside. He hurriedly left the manse grounds and returned home to Manordale. He was greeted by Lily who was waiting in the porch for him to return.

'Oh sir. I'm so pleased you've returned. There are two ladies waiting for you in the sitting room. I thought it best to put them there while they waited. It's Miss Susan Packham, she's only young, you know and oh, I almost forgot to mention there's a companion with her, a Miss Waterstone. I think they're the uninvited guests.'

'Thanks Lily. And the names tally. They are exactly who we were expecting to stay with us over the holidays. Now, you go and make some tea and bring it through to the sitting room and then you and Mrs

Hindmarsh and Mrs Whittaker, well you all take a break. You need it and deserve it. I'll leave my outside clothes in the study, take five minutes' breather and then I'll join them. Do you know if Emily has had time to finish preparing their rooms?'

'She's finishing off up there now.'

'Good. When she returns, she deserves a break as well.'

Jack turned and walked into his study. He read through the letter he had received from this long-time forgotten acquaintance and then tucked it into his jacket pocket before he went across to the sitting room to meet his 'Christmas company'. Whether he remembered them or not, they hadn't thought to telephone; they had just *'turned up'*.

Jack hoped that when he now met them, that things would progress on a better footing than the one on which they had begun.

Jack couldn't hide his look of surprise as he entered the sitting room; although he hoped the 'guests' did not notice. The two people who stood before him were total strangers to him. He was hoping that there would have been at least a glimmer of recollection dredged to the fore of his memory for the younger of these people, but it wasn't there, at all.

'I hope you haven't been waiting too long. I've been dealing with estate business. It always takes a little longer than one would anticipate,' Jack said.

The younger woman of the two stood up and offered her hand in a gesture of goodwill. 'It's so good of you to put us up for the next few weeks, and being so near to Christmas I was actually quite surprised when you agreed to take us on. And we haven't really kept in touch over the years have we, not since my father's death.'

'I must say I vaguely remember something of visits from your father, but of what actually happened, I have to say that it is a bit of a blank to me, and please do accept my apologies for that, but any friends of my father's will always be welcome at Manordale.'

'I am very grateful, anyway, and thank you. It's the Mayfair apartment, as I mentioned in my letter, it's woefully slow, the work that's being undertaken. The redecoration and the slight alterations that have been made and so on. I must say it's beyond me how the workmen, whoever they are, always seem to take so long over any type of job these days. Whatever it is they are doing.'

Jack nodded by way of reply.

A few minutes later Lily knocked at the door. Tea had arrived. Jack was pleased with the timing. 'Ah Lily, come along in. You can put the tray on the small table. I should introduce you to our first guests. They'll be here over Christmas and into the new year so you will become quite used to their faces around old Manordale.'

Jack then went on to introduce each to the other and salutations were exchanged between them. Before she left the sitting room Jack said, 'And Lily, when our guests are ready I'll ring for you, and if you wouldn't mind showing our guests their rooms?'

'As you wish, sir.'

'And Lily, go and take that break now, and try and relax.'

'I will, thank you, sir.'

Jack and the two ladies made polite small talk while they became acquainted with each other. Miss Susan Packham had some photographs with her that showed her visiting Manordale in the early 1900s. She looked about five or six years old. Miss Packham was quiet for a moment while Jack looked at the photographs and then she said, 'That was the year my mother died. Your mother and father were so very kind to us at a very sad time for me and Daddy and when we visited Manordale it was like a paradise. We stayed for a couple of weeks that summer. I remember it so very well.'

'You have a better recollection for these things than I seem to have,' Jack replied. Then there was a pause, perhaps only for a few seconds but it seemed like an eternity. Miss Susan Packham and Miss Waterstone looked at each other. A look of consternation appeared on their faces. Then, rather suddenly, Jack spoke, 'I thought up until the moment that I had heard you had arrived that I might be late for the Christmas party at the village school; which takes place tomorrow, before the children finish for the Christmas holiday. This year, I've arranged an extra treat for them; Father Christmas is going to make a surprise visit and give a gift to each of the children. Anyway, now you are here and I can get there for the start of the proceedings, I wonder, would you like to join me? We'll only be gone for a little over an hour and Grainger will take us in the car. We're to meet at Vale Court, the home of the Dennistoun Hardie's, around one-thirty, so we'll leave here at about a quarter past. What do you think?'

They both smiled. It was more than Jack expected, in fact. Then Miss Susan Packham spoke. 'That would be splendid. To be part of a real village Christmas.'

'That's settled then. We'll meet in the hall just before quarter past one and Grainger will have the car at the front, waiting for us.'

Susan smiled again. Christmas is going to be something to be enjoyed this year, even with all the upheaval, and that's all thanks to you, Jack.'

'As we're discussing events in the village and at Manordale, there's a tradition that's particularly special to Manordale, and I hope as dear to those who live and work here, as it is to me - and that's the masked ball on the 23rd of December. Everybody in the village is invited and a few others as well. Everyone who is invited, dresses up, fancy dress if they like, but so as no one knows who each other is, everyone takes a mask from the porch and puts it on before entering the hall proper; and the removing of cloaks is done at the very last minute, once you are in the hall, so absolutely no one has any idea who is hidden under the costume; or they shouldn't have at any rate. It's been going on since my late mother and father's time and I thought it was something that we should carry on with.'

'Sounds like it should be a hoot. What can we come as?' Miss Packham asked her companion, Miss Waterstone. Miss Waterstone didn't say anything, only smiled.

Jack thought the companion slightly strange. Perhaps a little too quiet but it could be that they had found the journey from London overlong and tiresome. Perhaps a visit to the village school tomorrow would make them more talkative. 'Would either of you like more tea?' Jack asked. Both Miss Packham and Miss Waterstone declined. Jack assumed that meant that they were ready to go to their rooms and he rang for Lily.

When Lily appeared she asked, 'Shall I take the tray, sir?' 'Please Lily,' Jack replied, 'but first I suppose you'd better show our guests to their rooms.' Lily nodded and smiled.

Jack looked at the two strangers before him. He was wondering how they would fit in with the Manordale way of doing things. Susan Packham looked at Jack, 'That would be a good idea, and then we could both freshen up and have a short rest.'

When Lily returned to collect the tray from the sitting room, Jack asked her if she would be able to visit Arthur at the hospital that evening. She said she would go for half an hour at seven-thirty. Jack told her that he would arrange for Grainger to drive her and wait for her at the hospital and then bring her home. Lily thanked Mr France and then she proceeded to remove the tray. 'Oh Lily, we never mentioned the dinner arrangements to our guests. Ask Emily to go up and tell them. It will be as usual, seven o' clock in the dining room.'

'Will you be dressing for dinner, sir. I'll need to let Emily know; in case the guests ask.'

'There's no need. Tell them this evening it's informal. That covers everything,' Jack replied.

Dinner passed rather pleasantly. The two guests were quite animated and were happy to discuss the ball and what they might wear. 'Remember it has to be kept secret. If you need any lengths of cloth or odds and ends to fashion something out of, please feel free to have a word with Lily or Mrs Hindmarsh. They will know where such things are to be found,' Jack said.

Jack told Miss Packham and Miss Waterstone more of the detail of the Manordale ball and how everyone, high or low was invited and that staff were brought in for the evening so the Manordale staff could have the time off, before the non-stop work over the Christmas and new year period.

'And I'm rather afraid we're adding to that work; and all because of your generosity towards us, which we do appreciate greatly. When the apartment's finished and you're in the Mayfair area, you must call in, please,' Susan Packham said.

'You might grow to regret the invitation. I'm often in London.'

'No. The invitation stands,' she replied.

'The Manordale ball, do you don fancy dress, Jack?'

'No, everyone but me. I try and arrange the hired staff and ensure everything runs smoothly. I rather enjoy it actually, truth be told.' There was laughter all round. The ice between Jack and his guests was beginning to break. He felt relieved. He offered his guests a drink and rose from the table to serve them. 'And Paris, from your letter Susan, I gleaned that you had lived in Paris for a time. What was Christmas like there? Very convivial, I expect.' Susan Packham was full of it. 'A place to be young all right. The clubs and the ever-popular jazz bars, everything, just everything in Paris had a spark about it and at Christmas that spark was almost a flame. The city went to town. The Metro was decorated with hundreds of tiny white lights and the streets too were similarly decorated; there were lights everywhere and the shops were an absolute sight to behold. They were a real invitation to spend money, whether or not you had it. It was also an especially nice time for the children. There were a lot of Christmas tableaux, everything lit up, all the figures. The ones with St. Nicholas on dressed in his red cape and with his sack of toys were very popular, and I must say the young children were agog, and some of the older ones, too. I suppose Hamley's puts on a decent display on Regent Street. It was always a draw when I was a child. The fact that you could try out some of the mechanical toys was what made it particularly special, to me at any rate.'

'Poor old Hamley's, it's been on a bit of a sticky wicket, lately. Trade has dipped badly, or so I heard. We'll have to wait and see what the new year brings but I expect Hamley's will be hoping for a good Christmas.

Hoping that the children have all been good, and that their parents are able to pay a hefty reward.'

'That's tough. I daresay Hamley's will come through the other side, though. They deserve too, I suppose. Anyway, back to Paris. I think you can tell from what I've said that I did enjoy the Parisian way of life.'

'They always used to say that it was the *'place to be seen'* , Jack said.

'There were a lot of people who went there just for that. In the summer Paris seemed to be filled with the good and the great.' Susan said.

'And did you ever see any of the French stars in Paris? I was only there in the summer. Late June early July, for the French Grand Prix. I was hoping to go and see a new singer, Maurice Chev. . .' before Jack had a chance to finish, they were interrupted by a knock at the door. Jack answered and found Lily standing before him. 'I'm sorry to interrupt you, sir, but I wanted to thank you before I go home. It was so kind of you to allow Grainger to drive me to the hospital. Grainger's taken the car back to the garage now, so I expect he'll be off in a few minutes and I'll just collect my things from downstairs and then I'll go, but I just wanted to say, 'thank you.'

'Pleased to help, Lily. Now no rushing off. I'd like to know, how is Arthur?'

'I left him smiling. So that's a positive note as I see it but the hospital staff won't give me a definite date for him to come home. But I know that I feel a lot better for having been able to see him. And I couldn't have done that easily without your help.'

'And Manordale wouldn't run so smoothly without you and Arthur. Don't forget that.'

Lily left and Jack went back to his guests. 'Now,' he said, 'shall we have that nightcap, and maybe we could carry on and chat about Paris.'

December 19th

The day dawned bright and clear and although there was a cold 'snap' in the air, it was quite pleasant. Any early-morning frost had all but disappeared.

Jack hoped that the children who would be finishing school today for the Christmas holidays would be excited when they had a visit from Father Christmas after their party. It was a surprise he hoped no-one at the school would anticipate. It had all been kept under wraps.

Jack had arranged with Grainger to drive himself and his guests across to Vale Court, so as to arrive by half past one, or thereabouts. He had asked young Terry Franks to be available to walk over and give a hand to Albert Riggs and walk back across to Vale Court with him. All Jack had to do was to remember to load the gifts into the car and to take the chocolate novelties with him. The morning was fairly quiet and Miss Packham and her companion were going to spend the morning walking in the grounds of Manordale. *'To do a little exploring,'* Susan had said. Jack had decided to take a walk past the Old Manse and then go on and have a quick word with Eileen Price, the churchwarden of St. Stephen's, who lived on the Nether Malting Road, almost opposite Albert Riggs cottage. He could easily fit both visits in this morning.

Jack France knocked on the cottage door. Eileen Price answered and then seemed quite taken aback when she saw that it was Mr Jack France standing on her doorstep. 'I didn't mean to surprise you, Mrs Price, but I just wanted a quick word. It's about the proposed carol service at St. Stephen's on Christmas Eve. I wanted to know if you had any idea how everything might be timetabled?'

'Oh, pardon me, Mr France, do come in, and you'd be surprised who's just stopped by, it's our new vicar, Reverend Smythe. And the service is the very thing we're discussing. Come on inside. I'll make some fresh tea.' Jack was ushered inside and introduced to

Reverend Smythe, before he was told to 'Sit, please!'. It seemed almost an order and Jack France did as he was summoned. No one in Moretondale had ever been seen to not comply with the demands of Mrs Eileen Price.

While Mrs Price busied herself in the kitchen the two men became acquainted. Jack apologised to Reverend Smythe for having missed him when he had visited the village a few days ago. Jack went on to say that he now had notification from the diocese and he thought that everyone in Moretondale was looking forward to the possibility of there perhaps being a Christmas service of some sort at St. Stephen's. Jack also said that he had contacted the former readers of the nine lessons and carols and they had all replied and indeed, were all available; he also said that he had heard through the grapevine that the choir were already practising. The organist, Mr Bolton was available and keen to go. He said that he expected Mrs Price would no doubt have word of the church ladies re flowers and cleaning.

'Did I hear my name mentioned?' Eileen Price said as she came back into the parlour of her cottage.

'You don't miss much, Mrs Price,' Reverend Smythe said, 'and that's a good quality for a churchwarden. I can see we will all get along famously.'

Mrs Price laughed and flushed slightly at the vicar's remarks but Jack could see that Mrs Price was relishing every minute, and Jack also wondered if he was included in the, *'we will all get along famously.'*

After a chat that lasted about forty-five minutes Jack decided it was time to get across to the Old Manse before heading back to Manordale. In that short space of time Jack had left Reverend Smythe in the capable hands of Mrs Price who at once agreed that she would forward all the relevant details pertaining to Mr Bolton and the carol service and she would get her ladies across to the church tomorrow so it would all be lovely for Christmas Eve. Jack could see that Reverend Smythe was pleased with the organisational skills of Mrs Price. Particularly when she said it would be her own personal task to distribute posters around the village advertising the event and also that she would personally contact all the readers and give them the required chapter and verse details.

Jack wondered whether he should say that he had told the selected readers that nothing would change since they last read at the service but decided against it. He didn't want to burst the bubble of Mrs Price's newfound delight at being 'in charge' of something again, so, he gave his farewells and turned to leave the two new friends in animated conversation. Perhaps this is just what Moretondale needs, he thought. *New people and some get up and go.* Jack smiled at the thought, and then turned again towards the sitting room before he was finally ushered through the cottage door by Mrs Price, but this time he glanced downward. It was then that something struck him. Why hadn't he noticed it earlier? Jack hoped that Reverend Smythe hadn't noticed the flash of realisation that had just shot across his face in that moment and then Jack quickly turned again and without another word, walked up the path and out into the lane. He didn't look back again.

Jack walked across to the Old Manse. He made the same checks as on his previous visits. Everything was as it had been. No sign of anything different or altered. And today, on both occasions he hadn't heard anyone reciting verses from the bible. He sighed, not knowing whether this was a sigh of relief or of frustration at all those things he didn't yet know. He left the grounds of the Old Manse and walked back up to Manordale, wondering if his mind had been playing tricks yesterday, and that he hadn't really heard anything at all; or was he perhaps making something out of nothing because it was what he wanted?

He also had concerns about the new incumbent, Reverend Smythe who he had just been introduced to by Eileen Price.

Later that Afternoon, Vale Court

Terry Franks set off early for Albert Riggs' cottage. He thought it would be for the best, and as he was always being told at home, '*Better to arrive early than get caught up in a problem that conspires to make you late.*' His mother, he thought, was the fount of all knowledge, up to a point.

Albert Riggs was ready and waiting on the step of his cottage when Terry arrived. 'Here you are, young man. And a relief to see you. I'll just lock the door and then we'll be off. It's always better to be early than be late out of a disaster occurring and you not having planned for the extra time.' Terry laughed. 'And what's that for?' Albert Riggs asked. Terry explained about his Mum and the two set off. 'I can see we're going to get on like a house on fire,' Albert Riggs said.

The two were early arriving at Vale Court but that didn't matter. They passed the time in chatting to Fred at the stables. Fred had the trap ready and Tess was already in harness. She was very calm and relaxed. Nothing, it seemed, would cause this filly to go into a state of fluster.

Albert spoke to Tess and stroked her muzzle. He said it was good to get to know animals. It reassured them to know that you were on their side.

Mr France hadn't yet arrived. Terry Franks said that he would take a walk along the drive and see if he could see anything of the car. He walked, with not a lot of haste, down the drive of Vale Court and to the main road. He stood for a few minutes looking up and down the road; there was no sign of the car.

Terry decided that he would walk a little further along the road, in the direction of Manordale. He had only gone a few yards when he heard the sound of a car horn and he turned to see Grainger, Mr France and his guests driving towards him up the road. Terry stood back to allow the car to pass him and then he watched as the car turned into the drive of Vale Court. He acknowledged them and turned to walk back up the drive and into Vale Court.

Jack walked round to the stables and handed the sacks of gifts to Albert, who placed them inside the trap. Then Terry got in and finally Albert, who settled himself in the driver's seat and then took the reins.

'Very nice. Very nice indeed,' Albert said as he readied himself for the short journey. He noticed the rug for his legs should the weather turn nippy and gave Mr France the 'thumbs up'.

Within ten minutes the trap et al, followed by Mr France's car were on their way to the school. The

Dennistoun Hardies stood waving their *'goodbyes'* from the stables.

At the School

When Jack France, Miss Packham and Miss Waterstone walked into the hall of the village school the children all 'ahhed' and oohed', and some children applauded. They knew that Mr France often carried chocolate into the Christmas party with him. They all looked eagerly to see if there was a hint of anything visible but there was not. Mr France went over to the headmistress. Miss James, and had a few words with her and the three members of school staff who, truth be told, looked a little frayed around the edges. Jack walked to the front of the hall, 'Now children, I know you must all be so excited as Christmas is a very special time of the year, and I might just say that you are all looking very smart and a credit to your parents and the school. And have you enjoyed all the Christmas food and lemonade and the games organised for you by Miss James and her staff?' There were shouts of 'YES', from the children. Jack France continued, 'I'm pleased that you are all having such a good time. Now, I would like to introduce my guests who are visiting with me at Manordale; please, step forward Miss Packham and Miss

Waterstone.' As Miss Packham and Miss Waterstone stepped forward they smiled at the children and said 'Hello'. Jack continued, 'Miss Packham and Miss Waterstone have travelled up to visit your school from London. Now children, who knows why London is so special, apart from our visitors who live there, of course?'

There were mixed callings out from the children of, *'Capital, The King, Mr Baldwin'.*

Mr France gestured with his hands to quieten the children and then he told them that it seemed to him that they knew everything there was to know about the city, so, before they finished their festivities and went home for the holidays he would go and see if he could find some chocolate in his car. There were more cheers from the children and the noise seemed to ring around the room.

Jack left the hall and went to the car where Grainger was waiting and he passed to Jack a sack containing the chocolate novelties, and at that same moment, as if on cue, Jack noticed the pony and trap turn into the school yard. Jack waited for them and then when Albert was ready, they walked into the hall, Terry Franks, carrying one of the toy sacks walked alongside Mr France. It made it less easy to see who was following behind. As they entered the school hall the children applauded. Miss Packham and Miss Waterstone were standing close to the staff and watched as Jack France and his entourage entered the hall.

Once they were close enough to the children Jack said, 'Now look who we found outside.' And then Jack and Terry separated so the children could see the man himself in his red and white garb. Again there were cheers and applause from the children. Miss Packham and Miss Waterstone applauded as well.

There was more applause and squeals of delight as the gifts were handed out to the children. After which Jack asked if any of them would like to come and see Father Christmas' sled. Hands flew upwards as the children indicated that they would. Jack left it to Miss James to split the children into groups. Albert Riggs, too, was full of the Christmas spirit and seemed to be enjoying every minute of the visit himself.

The visit to the school had been, in Jack's opinion, a resounding success.

Back at Manordale

It was almost three in the afternoon when Jack France and his guests arrived back at Manordale.

Grainger drove the car round to the garage and now his work began, the part he really enjoyed – getting the car 'put to bed' so to speak and ready for the next trip. The car was cleaned, inside and out. The final polish always took place directly before the car was needed. The chrome was polished until it shone like a mirror; the very act of doing this was something that filled Grainger with immense pride.

Inside the house, Jack escorted his guests to the sitting room and asked for some tea and light refreshments to be sent in. Jack, Susan and Miss Waterstone all chatted quite animatedly about how the afternoon had gone. Susan Packham and Miss Waterstone had really enjoyed their brief visit to the village school and meeting the children. 'We don't have the opportunity to do that type of thing much in London, I'm afraid. Everything is much too hectic, it seems. No time for the smaller details. Here, in the country, things seem so much more peaceful and easy-going. I feel we've appreciated the true meaning of Christmas at the school with the children this afternoon,' Susan Packham said.

When Lily came up to the sitting room sometime later to collect the tea tray, Miss Packham and Miss Waterstone were still deep in conversation. Jack said however, 'that he was pleased with Lily's timing as he needed her to ask Mrs Whittaker to come up to the study, straight away, he would like a word with her.' Lily explained that Mrs Whittaker would be finishing for the day at four o' clock. 'I know that, but I think this little diversion I have planned for her, she will jump at,' Jack replied. Lily smiled and left to go and find Mrs Whittaker. She did wonder though, what on earth Mr France could possibly have planned.

'Now Susan and Miss Waterstone, I will have to ask you to excuse me for a short while. I have a couple of telephone calls and a short visit to make and I am asking Mrs Whittaker if she will keep you company if you don't mind. She is a very loyal member of my staff and not only that, she is also very entertaining and knows everything there is to know about Moretondale and all the scandal that is happening, even in our town of Melford; and although she wouldn't admit it, both she and Maggie Evans from the shop could almost be twins. And I must go to see if she's ready. Excuse me, please.'

Jack went over to his study and went inside. A couple of minutes later there was a knock at the door. Jack opened it and saw Mrs Whittaker was waiting outside the study door. She looked slightly apprehensive and Jack smiled when he saw her. 'Don't worry', he said, 'there's nothing to worry about.' He held the door to let Mrs Whittaker go into the room before him. 'Now, come on, take a seat. I just want to ask you something.'

Jack put the idea to her. Mrs Whittaker sat quietly listening.

'So, that's it,' Jack said eventually, 'I would like you to just be some good old fashioned Manordale company for our guests. I have some business to attend to and I don't really like to leave them at a loose end for a length of time. I want them to feel looked after. You know all there is to know of Moretondale and I'm sure our guests will enjoy chatting with you.'

'And that's it? That's all I have to do?'

'That's all you have to do. And I expect to be home by around five o' clock, or just after, so you should be able to manage.'

'I'd love to help you sir. Thank you.'

Once Mrs Whittaker had been ushered into the sitting room, Jack gave his apologies and left. He wanted to have a word with Sir Cecil and he hoped that he wouldn't have gone off on some engagement or other. Jack was relieved when Jenkins answered the telephone and told him that Sir Cecil was at home. 'Oh Jack, it's you my boy. How are you?'

'I'm fine. I just wanted to ask you a few questions. There's something not quite right in Moretondale, but I'm not sure what it is, as everything on the face of it at least, is perfectly all right.'

Sir Cecil laughed. 'You haven't been drinking, have you, Jack?'

'No. just doing my good works as patron of the school and church. It's. . . , I wondered have you heard news of the new incumbent who's coming to take over at St. Stephen's?

'Yes and no. I haven't seen him but I have heard you'll have him there by January end.'

'Yes. That tallies with my letter from the diocese here. And the vicarage is in the middle of some redecoration before he arrives, so that's out of bounds. And the Old Manse, which first drew my suspicion is boarded up. That's taken place quite recently but as you perhaps know it's been empty ever since the fiasco and the burglaries this summer. The word is it will be going up for sale, but it isn't listed yet and no one saw who boarded it up, at least not in any detail.'

'Do you think it's possible that you're reading too much into past events?'

'No. And I'm certain of that and the new incumbent is Reverend Smythe. Have you heard of him?'

'The name's familiar. I'll see if I can find anything out, but it is Christmas in a day or two you know and people tend to start taking it easy, season of goodwill and all that. What I can tell you is that I do know I've never met anyone of that name.'

'Just see what you can do please. And the other thing is, do you still get the Standard?'

'I do. It should be dropping through the old letter box any minute.'

'And do you still read the *Londoner's Diary?*'

'It's where I find out all the best scandal, m'boy,' and Sir Cecil chuckled.

'I'm pleased to hear it. Has there been any mention of the Manordale Ball?'

'Not in the diary, but there was a small piece a few weeks ago, towards the end of November. There was a photograph of your father with some of his staff and a short write up. I didn't think to mention it to you when we last spoke as you know when the ball takes place. It's the same date every year.'

'That has been a great help, Sir Cecil. You don't know how much help. And don't forget, if you find anything about Reverend Smythe, let me know. And, as per usual, I'll speak to you on Christmas day.'

'Might not be back until late-ish Christmas morning. I'm one of the invited congregation for the recording of nine lessons and carols at King's College, Cambridge. I'm looking forward to it, I can tell you.'

'Same here, but we're hoping to pull something out of the hat for the village and perhaps do something in St. Stephen's. So, I'll leave everything now in your capable hands and we'll speak again soon.'

'We will, m'boy; don't worry.'

Jack sat for a few moments in the study digesting all that he had been told by Sir Cecil and then he took his hat and coat, readied his pipe with tobacco and set off for the *Ring o' Bells*.

It wasn't quite a quarter to five when he arrived at the *Ring o' Bells*. The pub wouldn't open until half past five. Jack could see the lights on at the back of the pub. The living quarters. Jack walked round to the side door and knocked. George Harris came to the door. 'Oh, Mr France, come in. We're just about to eat before we open up again at half-past five. Lucy's just in the kitchen. I'll go and tell her to wait a while before she dishes up.'

'Don't wait your meal because of me. What I've got to ask will only take a moment.'

'It's all right Mr France.' And George went off to find Lucy.

They both came into the back parlour together. Lucy was clad in a checked apron. She smiled as she said *'Hello'* to Mr France.

'George said there's something you'd like to ask us. I hope nothing's happened at Manordale,' Lucy said.

'No, but why should you say that. Has something been said in the village or in the pub?' Jack France asked.

'No. it's just a natural thought, I suppose. Anyway sit down and make yourself comfy for a minute or two.'

'Yes, sit yourself down Mr France,' George said, 'Now what was it you wanted to ask?'

'I just wondered whether you still had rooms here at the pub?'

George answered, 'Yes, just the two. They're not occupied so much as they used to be but we get people through enough to make it worthwhile.'

'And did anyone stay here towards the end of November, a man?'

'We did have one or two people stay over November time but I'm not sure of the date. Lucy, would you mind fetching the register from behind the bar.'

Lucy did as she was asked and returned a few moments later. She was already thumbing through the book. She ran her finger down the most recent pages.

'Ah, here we are, November 1st until the 6th, we had two guests; a lady, Mrs Gwendoline Baggott, she'd come to visit relatives down near Melford, the Baggotts who have a farm out towards the town, and a gentleman. Their stay overlapped a little. Mrs Baggott was with us until Tuesday the 6th. She left just before lunchtime and the gentleman was Mr Stephen Downey. He arrived on the 2nd of November, that was a Friday and left on the morning of Sunday 4th November. They were both rather quiet. Well, Mrs Baggott was out most of the time during her stay here visiting with her relatives. A short pre-Christmas visit I suppose. Delivering and exchanging of gifts and so on. And Mr Downey, he was only with us for those few days but when he arrived on the Friday he went out after eating his lunch here in the pub but on the Saturday he went straight out after breakfast and didn't return until about eight in the evening. And then of course he left the following morning, after breakfast. We didn't get to speak to either of them much apart from general chit-chat if they were in the bar area or at breakfast; you know the kind of thing, the weather and their Christmas plans so on.' Lucy looked to George for affirmation. He nodded in response. Lucy carried on, 'And then we'd no one until the 17th of November, that was a Saturday and that guest was with us all week. Leaving on the morning of the 24th as soon as they'd had breakfast. Seemed in a bit of a hurry. I thought they were probably going off to meet someone.'

'And who was that? A man or a woman?' Jack asked.

'Oh, sorry. It was a man. Mr Richard Smith.' He was out most of the time although he would chat to us and some of the regulars in the bar of an evening when he'd returned. He never ate here though, apart from breakfast.'

'Did he say why he was staying here?'

'Just on business,' George replied, 'but that's what a lot of folk say when they don't want to go into their own affairs too much with strangers. We hear it a lot.'

'How old was he?' Jack asked.

'I'd put him in his mid- to late fifties. He was always very polite and immaculately turned out. A real gent,' Lucy said.

'Anyone else stay at all?' Jack asked.

'No. That's it. Unless someone telephones on short notice for Christmas or new year that will be that for us until 1929,' George said.

'You've helped me more than you can know,' Jack replied, 'and I'll leave you to have your meal before it spoils and I'll head off back to Manordale for mine.'

Later that Evening

Jack walked quickly home to Manordale. He had spent longer with the Harris's than he anticipated and he thought that he should now return to rescue Susan Packham and Miss Waterstone from Mrs Whittaker's care. He had also been thinking over what Sir Cecil and the Harris's had said. He was sure there was something funny going on at the Old Manse, and whatever was being planned was going to happen soon. Perhaps over the Christmas celebrations; when it would perhaps be least expected.

When Jack arrived home and walked into the hall he was immediately greeted by Lily. She was smiling. Jack removed his hat and coat as he spoke. 'You look happier than you did earlier in the day, Lily. Good news from the hospital?'

'Yes. Exactly that. They are going to let Arthur come home tomorrow. They'll bring him in an ambulance and he'll have a wheelchair until he can get around using the crutches they've sent. They say he won't have to go back to see the doctor until after Christmas while they just check on the plaster and how everything's going.'

'I'm pleased that it's all turned out all right. And if I can leave you to see to my hat and coat, I'll go and take over from Mrs Whittaker and give my guests some relief.'

'Oh no, Mr France, don't worry about your guests. They've all been getting on famously. They've had enough tea and scones to sink a ship. And every time I've been up to the sitting room they've been laughing – in the main at Mrs Whittaker's jokes!'

'I'll go and spoil their fun then. And thank you Lily. Dinner at seven for three in the dining room?'

'Yes, Mr France. Thank you.'

Jack left Lily and went into the sitting room to take his chance.

'Good evening,' Jack said as he opened the door and walked through to join them. 'Mrs Whittaker has kept you entertained I hear?'

Susan Packham And Miss Waterstone nodded. Susan Packham said brightly, 'Most definitely. A very entertaining lady.'

Jack thought he noticed Mrs Whittaker blush, ever so slightly.

December 20th

Jack breakfasted in the dining room, alone. Miss Susan Packham and Miss Waterstone had both decided to breakfast in their rooms. They were both sure that they were coming down with *something,* though what that *something* was, neither of them was certain. They both had slightly different symptoms, according to Mrs Hindmarsh who informed Mr France of the facts of their malady when she checked in the dining room to make sure everything was all right for him. 'All right?' he questioned. 'Mrs Hindmarsh, may I say that no one can devil a kidney quite like you. Everything is delicious.'

Mrs Hindmarsh thanked Mr France and then went back downstairs to check on what Mrs Whittaker and Emily were up to.

Mrs Hindmarsh found them both chatting about costumes for the ball. She felt that she should reprimand them but then decided against this. It was Christmas coming up after all and they were both keen to get on with their costumes, as she was. Mrs Hindmarsh took a vacant chair at the table and joined in with the conversation.

In the dining room Jack was considering all that he had discovered yesterday. As his guests were incapacitated

Jack thought he would go and pay a call on Mrs Price and Albert Riggs and see if there was anything of note going on around the Old Manse. It was involved in some way with whatever was going to happen. He was becoming more certain of it than ever. Jack was also hoping to hear something from Sir Cecil, before he was off to Cambridge on Christmas Eve. If he didn't hear from him prior to the 24th, Jack felt it might be too late.

Jack rang down and asked that Emily might be sent up to the dining room, to clear the breakfast things away and also clean the sideboard. He wanted it dealing with as soon as possible in case any other of the guests arrived. They weren't expected, but one could never tell.

When Emily arrived at the dining room she knocked on the door before entering, and then walked rather timidly inside. 'I've come to clear the breakfast things for you,' she said. 'Yes Emily, that's fine, but just come and sit down for a moment. I would like a quick word with you.'

'Yes sir,' she replied.

'Yes. Now I have to go out for a little while this morning and I shan't be back before lunch. Now as you might know, our two guests are a little under the weather this morning so I'd like you to be their personal assistant for this morning. They might want drinks and so on, and you will have to clear their rooms as well, so

I would suggest that if an hour has passed and they haven't rung down for anything, you should go and check on them. It's a bit of a damp squib in all respects to be ill or off colour at this time of the year. A time of the year when happiness and fun is going on all around you, so I would like them to feel well looked after, here at Manordale.'

'Yes sir,' Emily replied.

'That's the ticket. Now Emily, do you happen to know if young Terry Franks is anywhere on the estate this morning?'

Emily smiled. 'He was with Grainger, earlier. They were in the garage and working on the Avis, I think.'

'Oh, good. Right, I'll leave you to get on with your work Emily and I'll go and see if Terry Franks is available to come out with me this morning; and don't forget, you're in special charge of our guests.'

'Yes sir. Thank you.'

'Now, I'm going to go across and have a word with Lily, to see if there's been any word on Arthur from the hospital and after that I'll go and see if I can find Terry Franks.'

Lily was busying herself getting the cottage ready for when Arthur arrived back home. The ambulance wasn't expected until after 2 o'clock. She had plenty of time and Mr France had said she must leave everything at Manordale in the capable hands of Mrs Hindmarsh and Mrs Whittaker, and that if she needed any help with anything at all she was to ask, and if needs be, Emily would be able to come over to the cottage and give a hand. Lily wondered just how capable Mrs Whittaker was; but kept her thoughts to herself and also chided herself for the spiteful thought she had just had, when she was the one being offered help.

When Mr France had left the cottage, Lily thought that she might spend some of the free time she had while waiting for Arthur's return, on her costume for the ball as it was only three days away now.

She had yards of various fabrics from dresses she had made for herself over the years. It was just an idea she was short of. Arthur was also on her mind and that was of course, only to be expected but she was thinking whether or not he would be able to attend the ball. There was no point in him being masked, though. Everyone would know that it was Arthur – the wheelchair alone would be a giveaway. She decided she would wait until Arthur arrived back home and give him some time to get settled before getting his thoughts on the event. It had to be his decision but she would much rather keep an eye on him at Manordale, than he be left alone in the cottage.

Jack found Terry Franks at the garage with Grainger as Emily had said he would. Mr France explained that he would like Terry to join him while he carried out some estate business. Terry Franks smiled. He felt that perhaps he was being taken seriously at Manordale at last. He would have liked to be at Manordale full time, and not only as and when. Maybe this could be the beginning of that.

Jack France and Terry Franks walked along the road towards Albert Riggs cottage together. Terry was struggling to keep up with Jack. When Jack was going somewhere with a purpose in mind he was always on the move. If anyone had asked, he would have said that if you wasted time you ended up with wasted days, and he would have none of that. 'Do you enjoy the work you get at Manordale?' Jack asked, as they walked along. 'Yes. And I like helping Grainger with the cars. Working with Riley's all right but I don't think he'll ever make a gardener out of me.'

Jack laughed, 'Well at least you're being honest, and that's always good. Whoever you are speaking with, honesty is always the best policy. Of course, there are times when you have to do slightly the opposite, but we'll not dwell on that at the moment. Part of the reason I've asked you along today is because I'm going to see Albert Riggs and Mrs Price, the churchwarden, but I also want to have a look around the grounds of the Old Manse; and I think another pair of eyes and ears would be useful.'

Terry beamed at Mr France. 'I'm pleased to be of assistance, sir. Thank you.'

'Come on, let's hurry along and see what Mr Albert Riggs is up to.'

Within ten minutes they were inside Albert's cottage. The fire was blazing away and Jack wondered how the old man stood the heat in his small cottage.

'Now, what can I help you with today. You don't want me to be Father Christmas anywhere else, do you?'

'No, nothing like that.'

'That's good then as I wouldn't be up to it at the minute as I seem to have misplaced my black boots. They'll be here abouts somewhere but I can't put my finger on them at the moment.'

'What did you just say, Albert?'

'Nothing really. I just can't place where I've put my boots, my black ones.' He lifted his leg slightly, 'You see these ones are my brown boots. My everyday boots. My black boots are my *special occasion* boots.'

'Albert, don't ask me to say any more, but what you've just said has been a great help. Thank you. And now, the real purpose of my visit; I just want to find out all you know about the comings and goings at the Old Manse within the last few weeks, possibly since mid-November.'

Albert sat down and hummed and ahhed a few times. 'That's one to think about Mr France. I told you I didn't see who exactly boarded the doors and windows up. They weren't faces I knew but I saw a few men around the grounds but that wouldn't be earlier than perhaps the end of November, or the last week maybe. It definitely was before December. It was all done and boarded by then.'

'And did you notice anyone that you might be able to give a description of, or a feature that you remembered of any of the men there?'

'Three or four of the men looked like jobbers. Those who take whatever work they can. They might not do a fancy job but they do a job when it's needed, and probably at short notice. You know the type of men I mean?'

'I get the idea. So, did one of them look like the boss?'

'Oh yes. I watched from my window and a man who looked quite smart and respectable drove into the grounds of the manse and left with the other men in the car. I don't know where they went, mind.'

'The man you took to be the boss, how old about would you say he was?'

'I'm not good on ages, sir, he was dark haired though, just a tinge of grey; but age-wise, he was older than you and a lot younger than me. That's all I can say, really.'

'That's fine Albert. I only need to know what you saw.'

'And that's what I'm telling you, sir.'

'Have any of them or anyone else been back to the Old Manse recently?'

'No. I haven't seen a soul and I told you, I went to Leigh's in Melford, thinking it might be up for sale, but if it is, it's not with them.'

'Yes. That's what I heard when I telephoned.'

'Do you think something's wrong there sir?'

'Perhaps not wrong, Albert, but then not quite right, either.'

'That's a conundrum, that is.'

'Perhaps Albert, but when you have chance, could you make a note of any activity you see? If you see anyone going into the manse grounds; even if it's only the postman, take a note, and the date and time would be useful as well.'

'As you wish, sir. Of course. Anything to be of help.'

'Right, well young Franks and I will leave you now and after I've called in to see Mrs Price, Franks and I will be going into the manse grounds, and there's no need to add us to any list,' Jack said, and then he and Terry Franks left the cottage.

'Do you think there is something going on at the Old Manse, sir?' Terry Franks asked as they walked up to Mrs Price's cottage.

'I'm not sure. It's just an inkling I have and I need to find out for my own peace of mind,' Jack answered.

Jack knocked on Eileen Price's door and was pleased to find her at home. 'Oh, come on inside sir, and you, young Terry come in and find a seat by the fire, it's a cold one today.'

'It is,' Jack said. Terry Franks smiled and doffed his cap.

'I was about to put the kettle on. Would you both like a cup of tea?'

It was agreed they would have tea and Mrs Price busied herself in the kitchen and a little while later a veritable feast on a tea tray found its way into the parlour. 'You'll both have room for a slice of cake, I 'spect?'

Terry Franks said 'Yes', straightaway. He didn't want the cake to find its way back to the kitchen. Jack France nodded, and then added, 'Thank you very much, Mrs Price.'

When Mrs Price had completed her duties as hostess, she asked Mr France the purpose of his visit, pleasant though it was.

He asked the same questions of her that he had asked of Albert Riggs. Mrs Price hadn't seen anyone but as she asserted to Jack France, she didn't *spend all her days looking through the windows*. She had *plenty of other things to do that occupied her time.*

Mr France said that he knew she was very busy, particularly now that St. Stephen's was to welcome a new vicar in the new year and with the carol service having to be put together at such short notice she would have a lot on her plate at the moment.

'I have a lot of help with the church duties. Everyone has been so helpful and generous with their time,' she said.

'That's no less than I would expect from the residents of Moretondale,' Jack replied.

Mrs Price picked up some knitting that she had put on a side table when her visitors arrived. 'I'm knitting a little coat for my niece's baby,' she said, 'a little boy.'

'It's a very intricate pattern and fine wool. It will take care and time,' Terry said.

'Oh, and how do you know that?' Mrs Price asked.

'My Mum does a lot of knitting. I knit a little myself when I have the time.'

Mrs Price looked at Terry. 'I'm amazed. I truly am. I wish more people would knit. It's quite relaxing, but with this at the moment, it isn't,' she said, holding the knitting aloft, it's a Christmas gift and I should be knitting for the rest of the day just to get it finished and ready; I dare say.'

'Well don't let us detain you,' Mr France said as he stood up, followed by Terry, 'but if you notice anything or anyone in the grounds at the Old Manse, would you keep a note of it?'

Mrs Price hmphed. 'I'll see what I can do,' she said.

Jack and Terry smiled. 'Thank you', Jack said, and the two of them left the cottage and walked across to the Old Manse.

'Excuse me, sir, What are we doing here. It's all boarded up?'

'I know,' Jack France replied, 'but it's why it's boarded up that bothers me. No one seems to know the reason why. And no one seems to know *who* was responsible. It may be nothing at all but I think it is fishy. And if a thing seems fishy, then it usually is.'

'Mum says it's going up for sale.'

'A lot of people in the village have mentioned that to me as well but it isn't up for sale yet. People, you see, observe only what they think they *see*. They don't actually *look*.'

'You've lost me a bit there, Mr France, but all I see here is a boarded-up house, well, manse to be correct and covered over are all the downstairs windows and doors. It looks empty. No one is about the property except us, here in the grounds and there are no lights visible in the upstairs windows, as far as I can tell, from the outside.'

'There you are then, Terry. You're doing just what I've told you people do, only a moment ago. You are observing what you *think* you see. You're not looking.'

'I am?'

'You are.'

The two walked in silence around the grounds of the Old Manse. Terry, every few yards looked at Mr France to see if he could glean anything from his expression. Terry gleaned nothing. Mr France just walked and then stopped for a moment and occasionally took his pipe from his coat pocket, before returning it again; he didn't even attempt to light it. It was as if he couldn't make up his mind whether or not he was going to smoke it, or there again, whether he thought that it might help him in his attempt to come up with a theory. This performance carried on for a few minutes before Jack

France broke the silence. 'Notice anything unusual?' he asked Terry Franks.

'No. I don't think so.'

'Did you look down at the flower bed by the front porch?'

'No. I just glanced, sir. I didn't know I was supposed to be looking.'

'You always have to be observant, Terry. That's how you discover what you were never expecting to find.'

'Yes sir,' Terry replied. And he looked at Jack France and wondered what on earth was going on in his head and what he was supposed to do to help.

Jack France and Terry walked round to the front porch. Jack stopped in front of the flower bed. 'Now Terry, look here in the soil,' and Jack pointed to footprints. 'These weren't here the last time I walked the manse grounds, so, that must mean . . . ,'

'…that someone else has been here in the meantime,' Terry interrupted.

'Exactly. Now you're getting on the same wavelength as me. The thing is, it is things like this, however trivial they may seem, that are so very important.'

'I can see that, Mr France, all of it.'

Jack France knelt down to take a closer look at the footprints. 'What do you think? What would you say on your first real looking at these footprints, Terry. Have a go.'

Terry knelt down. 'They're not too small, and they're not really large prints. Could that make them a young man or small adult man?'

'I suppose it could. Have you a piece of paper and a pencil handy?'

Terry ferreted around in his jacket pocket, found the required items and immediately drew the shape and gave an approximate size of the footprints and where they were found. Jack glanced down. 'Good work Terry,' he said.

From the flower bed, the two went around the house checking all the boarded-up doors and windows. They were all secure and you couldn't see inside the property. Jack and Terry then walked to the back of the house and the old coal house. Jack pulled the door open and the pair looked inside. It was as it had been previously. Nothing was moved or changed. 'It's pretty dark in there,' Terry said. 'And if anything isn't right, it's in there.'

'What do you mean?'

'Where the pile of coal is piled up against the corner, it's covering something. Perhaps a coal chute to send it directly to the cellar if they were having coal delivered for the boilers for heating the water. A lot of the big houses have them now.'

'I'd never thought of that! That's what a pair of young eyes do, you see. And how do you know about boilers and hot water?'

'My Uncle Eric. He's a plumber. And as he says, *He's doing very nicely thank you and all thanks goes to the uptake and installation of the new-fangled, coal-fired, hot water boiler.'* Terry smiled. 'I'm pleased to hear it,' Jack France replied.

Jack decided that there was probably enough time to take a closer look at the inside of the coal shed. Terry had been correct. Once the coal was moved a little further back the opening to a chute appeared. It had obviously been at one time a flight of stone steps going down into the cellar; perhaps there as a means to get into the cellar from the garden if needs be and probably meant for use by the staff. That would have been in the recent past when the property was last in use as a manse. The chute had been added when the boiler was installed, making use of the steps that were previously there. It wouldn't take much effort or thought to add some sort of concrete over the steps to form a ramp, and to then add a wooden hatch cover and then of sorts you had your chute. The cover only needed to be opened when there was a delivery of coal. It was plausible enough. Jack ran the thoughts through his head. Whoever was up to something now, knew the layout of the Old Manse; and that could only mean that it must be someone from the village, and a long-time resident at that; or someone who had at one time or another lived in Manordale and knew the recent history of the manse.

Jack France closed the door of the coal shed and left everything as he had found it. Jack and Terry walked around the grounds again. 'Look up, Terry, and look if you can see anything in the upstairs windows.'

Terry looked up, straining his eyes to the point that they began to prick and burn in the chill air but there was nothing visible.

Jack France looked at his wristwatch. It was almost twelve-thirty. 'We'd better finish up here now, and head off back to Manordale.'

December 20th, 2 p.m.

Inside the cottage on the Manordale estate, Lily was anxiously waiting for Arthur's return. If Arthur had been home he would have been telling her '*To stop wearing the carpet out.*' She could hear Arthur's voice in her head. It caused her to smile.

Miss Packham and Miss Waterstone were still incapacitated. Emily's duties as maid of all work and nursemaid to the sick, was extended until supper time.

In his study, Jack was mulling over the events of the morning at the Old Manse, doing a mental review of everything he knew.

While he had been at the Old Manse with Terry, he hadn't heard anyone reciting prayers or verses from the bible. He did, however, conclude that Terry Franks had been of some immense help with his remarks about the fad for water-heating boilers that was sweeping the rural parts of the country. Jack knew that heating boilers for the home were very popular in London and other towns and cities throughout the country but in more rural areas just having hot water to wash or bathe in available at the turn of a tap, was a boon.

Manordale hadn't gone that far yet. The old copper survived in one of the outbuildings, and it was still in working order but Jack France was considering the installation of a coal-fired heating boiler. Hot water whenever it was required, and perhaps heating throughout the house. Now that would be something to be desired. The colder mornings of winter made it suddenly appear quite compelling. And Jack was one for modernisation, and new gadgets, whatever they were, were also worthy of consideration. Jack would never give up on tradition but he wouldn't want to be left behind in the race for modernity, either.

Jack thought that another visit to the Old Manse might be in order and he decided that he would go this afternoon; as soon as he could after Arthur Graves was brought home from the hospital. He would also like a brief word with Arthur and Lily before he went off to do anything else but with the light fast fading, Jack knew that if Arthur's return was delayed, there wasn't much hope of him getting across to the Old Manse before in any sort of daylight.

Jack sat for a few minutes more and then decided he would go downstairs to see how Emily and Mrs Hindmarsh were getting along before he went over to the Graves' cottage to have a word with Lily and see if there had been any news from the hospital.

Mrs Hindmarsh and Emily were busy preparing titbits for the Christmas celebrations. 'Any news of our invalids?' Jack enquired.

'Nothing's changed as far as I can see,' Emily said. 'They seem to be taking plenty of drinks. Mrs Hindmarsh sends up hot, sweet, lemon tea with every tray.'

'It's the only thing if you're off colour,' Mrs Hindmarsh said.

Emily smiled. 'I'm really looking forward to the Christmas ball, Mr France. I want to see if I can guess who the people are behind the masks and in their costumes.'

'It's great fun,' Jack replied. 'And, Mrs Hindmarsh, the caterers and their staff have asked if they might have the kitchen to prepare the food on the 23rd. I have told them as long as they don't arrive before two o'clock, it shouldn't be a problem. I know how you like to clear up after lunch before the 'staff' come into your kitchen.'

'That will be fine,' Mrs Hindmarsh replied, 'and I'm looking forward to the ball as well. And you know I absolutely enjoy how we, the Manordale staff can do our own little bit of dressing up the ballroom for the occasion. We've been spending some of our free time making up little baubles and painting bits of greenery we managed to get from Mr Riley. Emily's been sticking glitter on the leaves. A bit of a mess that caused, I can tell you.'

Jack France laughed quietly. 'I can imagine,' he said, and then added, 'I must leave you two to your work and I'll go and catch up with Lily. Excuse me, ladies.'

Jack walked to the Graves' cottage and tapped on the door. Jack waited for her to answer. 'Ah Lily, just a quick word with you if you don't mind.'

'No, of course Mr France, come in.'

Jack sat down and waited for Lily to join him. 'I wondered if you'd heard any more about Arthur. It's about time he was home, isn't it?'

'Yes. Yes, and he's on his way. It took a while for them to get him fastened in and then the wheelchair was little bit awkward, I believe, but I'm expecting him very shortly and I hope to find him in good shape. It was such a relief to me to visit him, I can tell you. And thanks again for all your help.'

'I'm pleased to hear that he's at last on his way home. I was hoping to get to the Old Manse again, if I could, before the light fades altogether but then I'd also hoped to see Arthur on his return.'

'Sir, please don't miss doing what you have in mind on our account. I'll have to get him settled into the cottage when he's first home and that might take longer than expected. I've made a put-up bed in the sitting room. He won't be able to do stairs, and I wouldn't want him to, even if he could.'

'I wanted to see what you thought first, Lily. So, I'll get off to the manse now and call in again on my return and hopefully Arthur will be able to recuperate in your good care.'

Jack left Lily and set off for the manse. He took a torch with him and walked quickly along the short distance. He first checked the flower bed by the porch. The footprints were still there. He walked around the perimeter of the grounds and then went across to the coal shed. It was as he and Terry Franks had left it earlier. He took the shovel that was propped up outside the shed and began to move the coal away from the corner of the coal shed. It took a little while but soon he saw fully the entrance to a chute. The cover once lifted would reveal the chute where the coal could be dropped down into the cellar. There was a chain and a padlock keeping the chute entrance fastened. It was locked. Jack didn't have a key with him and cursed himself at his ineptitude. He held the torch close to the padlock and checked the make. It was difficult to make out the name that was stamped on the metal. It was worn and looked as though there was a 'J' or it could have been an 'I', impressed at the top. It was obviously a padlock that had had a previous life. Jack decided that he would go into Melford as soon as he was able the following day and see if Mr Sykes at the hardware shop sold such locks, and if so, whether there were spare keys available.

Jack shovelled the coal back to its original place and closed the door of the coal shed. He replaced the shovel to the exact same place he had taken it from. Satisfied that everything was as it should be, he left the Old Manse and walked back to Manordale.

Jack washed and changed when he arrived home. The coal dust seemed to have got everywhere. He could both smell it and taste it.

He checked the time; it was 3.30 p.m., Jack went straight across to Arthur and Lily's cottage and knocked on the door.

Lily answered. 'Oh, Mr France, come in and sit down if you can find a seat. It's been all go since the ambulance men left, and they were a great help to me, I can tell you. They have Arthur all settled.' Jack turned to see Arthur propped in a large armchair, his leg raised on a highish stool.

'They've let you out at last, then?' Jack asked.

'At last,' Arthur replied. 'Mind you sir, only hours ago I wasn't sure how it would go and I definitely didn't want to be in the hospital at Christmas. And I didn't want to miss the ball, either. I'm still invited I hope?'

'Of course. As long as you're able to come and it won't cause a problem to you in any way. We don't want any more surprises of the accidental kind; but if you are at all able it will be my pleasure to see you at Manordale. In fact, if you're able to come, I'll come over and push you across in your wheelchair.' Jack turned and gestured to the chair which had been placed behind a sofa in the Graves' sitting room.

Arthur said, 'I'll make sure I'm there. I think the mask and fancy dress is out for me this year but I'll stay on the sidelines as it were. I don't want to get in the way with my leg. It has to be kept slightly raised.'

'The chair has a little piece that pulls out at the front,' Lily said, 'it's ever so clever.'

'Now, is there anything I can do for you? Anything you need from the house?'

'We're being well looked after Mr France. Mrs Hindmarsh has promised to send Emily over with some hotpot for our supper.'

'Everything's under control, then,' Jack said, and he left the Graves' cottage and returned to Manordale.

Jack had his meal in his study. His guests ate in their rooms. They had sent word with Emily to the effect that they hoped to be up and about as normal in the morning.

After a few minutes, Jack closed his eyes and rested his head on the wing of the chair. He was soon asleep and remained so until a quarter past eight. He hadn't felt particularly tired when he sat down but felt more refreshed when he awoke.

The sleep had obviously been rewarding in more ways than one. He now thought that he may have some idea on what was happening; or going to happen, and perhaps where it might happen. He had woken to see things more clearly. In the morning he would again visit the Old Manse, and then drive over to Melford and check up on specific makes of padlock. And perhaps later, after lunch, he might call in and see Inspector Paxton. Yes, there was a light shining on the problem now, and he was beginning to understand those things that hadn't yet presented themselves.

December 21st, Morning

Jack and Grainger were ready to set off early for Melford. Terry Franks was busy helping Riley in the grounds, which wasn't the job he had hoped for when Mr France came round to the garage earlier in the morning.

Jack had heard from Mrs Hindmarsh that Miss Packham and Miss Waterstone were reportedly feeling much better when Emily had checked on them earlier when she had taken in their breakfast trays, and indeed, they were both expecting to be down for lunch in the dining room. Emily thought that of the two ladies it was Miss Waterstone who sounded a little more croaky.

That gave Jack very little to be concerned about regarding the Manordale guests, which was good news at any rate; and so when he returned to Manordale later, he thought he might go along to the Graves' cottage and see if they were in need of anything now that Arthur was back home. He imagined that things might present themselves suddenly when you were dealing with those in a period of convalescence.

'How is everything with the cars?' Jack asked Grainger as they drove along to the Old Manse.

'Everything in good order. And if you're asking as tomorrow is the 22nd and I might have trains to meet for the guests coming over for the ball; I can assure you Mr France, that it is all in hand.'

'You'll be there on the 23rd I take it?'

'Yes sir. The costume ball is the one event in the year that I will always give my visit to the *Ring o' Bells* up for.'

Jack smiled. 'Thank you, Grainger. We may as well drive up to the Old Manse, inside the drive gates, I mean, and then you can come with me. I want to pick your brains.'

'As you please, sir.'

Once inside the Old Manse grounds the two men walked around the outside of the manse and then Jack decided they should walk over to the front porch flower bed. Jack told Grainger about the footprints that were there when he had visited with Terry Franks. Everything was as Jack had left it. The footprints were still there, albeit less defined than they had been the previous day. Jack and Grainger then walked on to the back of the manse and the old coal shed. 'Young Terry Franks spotted something interesting in here yesterday. To do with the hot water boiler for the manse.' Jack France opened the coal shed door and showed the pile of coals to Grainger. 'Underneath the coal there's what seems to be an entrance. Terry reckons it's a chute for sending coal down for the boiler. I took another look at it late yesterday afternoon. It would appear that young Franks is correct. It would have already been an entrance to the cellar, perhaps for those working in the manse grounds to gain access to the house without going through the front entrance or the back, which would have meant going through the main hall or the kitchen area. It would have been quite a simple job to adapt the original steps and put on a cover to prevent mishaps but that would also allow coal to be dropped into the cellar, to stoke the new boiler, whenever it was needed. The padlock's a mystery though, can't make out the name. It's obviously not the first place it was used but there doesn't seem to be a key anywhere and it's locked fast.'

'I'd agree with you, sir. And young Terry's probably right. I believe the manse was modernised for the hot water before the Methodist church closed and the minister moved on. I also believe the property's up for sale.'

'Have you been in the newsagents and spoken to Maggie Evans, by any chance?' Jack asked.

'She told me the bit about it going up for sale but I know that the manse was modernised by the church, ready for the new minister who would be coming in but with the numbers in the congregation dropping, eventually, as you know the church closed. All the Moretondale Methodists have to go into Melford now.'

'I should pay more attention to what's going on in the village,' Jack said, 'then I might be up to date with all the local gossip. Anyway, regarding the manse, it wasn't up for sale the last time I checked with Leigh's in Melford but I am aware that the manse being for sale is the rumour that's spreading around Moretondale.'

'It's been boarded up a week or two now though. Isn't that a sure sign? I mean they do it with these big old buildings to protect the windows and also to stop people from gaining access.

'To be honest Grainger I'm not sure what's going on except that things have a strange odour of fish about them.'

'Yes sir.'

Jack and Grainger walked around the manse again, Jack hoping that they would hear something, but they didn't. At one point Grainger thought he saw a shadow through one of the upstairs windows but then thought better of it and suggested that it might be no more than a trick of the light and perhaps the branches of the trees that bordered the perimeter of the manse grounds giving an idea of a human reflection. As before, Jack suggested one final check at the back of the property and the coal shed. Nothing was unusual. It was all as it had first been found.

The two men left and set off on the short drive into Melford. It would only take about ten minutes.

On arriving in Melford, the car pulled up outside Sykes' hardware shop. Jack went inside while Grainger stayed with the car.

'Mr Sykes, just the man I need to speak to,' Jack said as he entered the shop.

'Oh. Happy to be of assistance, Mr France. Anything in particular that requires my advice?'

'Actually, yes. There's a padlock on one of the old outhouses at Manordale and we seem to have misplaced the key. I wondered, are keys interchangeable on padlocks, and if so, perhaps just a new key would suffice or perhaps two, in case we lose any more.'

'Now Mr France, it could be yes and it could be no. Some locks, like suitcase locks and such, you do find that the keys, they are interchangeable but with padlocks it's different. They're more of a security feature as a general rule, so out of every hundred or perhaps every thousand keys you might find one and although it won't be an exact match, with a bit of forcing you might be able to undo a padlock with it.'

'Oh. I was hoping for better news than that. I suppose that means we may have to fall back on the chain cutters then, as it were.'

'It would appear so, sir.'

Jack smiled and left Mr Sykes' shop. He hadn't really learned anything more and in that respect he felt as though it had been a wasted visit.

Grainger was waiting by the car as Mr France approached and he opened the door to let him get in.

'Not quite ready yet, Grainger. I'll just call in at Leigh's and see if there's any news on the status of the Old Manse; and I'll walk. You could stay with the car. It will only take me a minute or two to get there. And then remind me in case I forget, to ask on my return about the previous Methodist minister and when he left the property.

Jack walked over to the office of Leigh's and was quite pleased when he saw Mr Leigh in the front office. It saved Jack asking for him.

'Mr France. Good to see you. And how may we help you this morning?'

'Just being a nosey neighbour. Any news on the manse. Is it up for sale yet?'

'Not just yet. And I'm not supposed to let anyone in on this but I'm hoping it will be on our books when we re-open in the new year.'

'That is good news.'

'Yes. So, if you're interested in the property come in as soon as the festivities are over and I might be able to arrange a viewing. We should have the keys to the property then, all being well.'

Jack realised that Mr Leigh was under the impression that he was speaking with a potential client and he felt it only a courtesy to let Mr Leigh know that he wasn't really interested in purchasing the property. Jack rambled a little and then told Mr Leigh that he found Manordale time consuming enough and that he wasn't a prospective buyer in waiting.

Mr Leigh's face dropped. He felt that he had been taken for a ride and was none too pleased. 'If that's all then, Mr France,' he said, 'some of us *do* have work to do.'

Jack joined Grainger at the car. He relayed the story to him of what had taken place in Leigh's office and then asked Grainger about the Old Manse and if he had any idea of the time when the Methodist minister had left Moretondale and moved into Melford.

'I'm not really familiar with the Old Manse at all and if I go anywhere, it's St. Stephen's but I've a feeling Mrs Whittaker had a dalliance with the Moretondale Methodist church at one time and she might be able to give you the details on that. And if not Mrs Whittaker, you could always call in and see what idea Maggie Evans has on things.'

Jack looked at his wristwatch. 'It's barely ten-thirty now,' he said. 'I think we'll call at Maggie's shop on the way over to Manordale.'

Jack went into Maggie's shop while Grainger, yet again, waited with the car. Jack asked all the relevant questions and was pleased with Maggie's reply. 'Now let me see,' she said. 'It must be about three years ago. I didn't attend the church but I used to go along to the Ladies' meeting that was held in the front room of the Old Manse on Monday afternoons. It was good to catch up with everyone in the village and exchange chat. Anyway, the minister's wife, Jocelyn, she happened to remark that if the numbers attending didn't start going up, there was danger that the church might close and the congregation, such as it was, would have to join up with the Methodist church in Melford. The church was only small anyway, you couldn't really fit many in. In fact, I'd swear that the manse was a lot bigger than the church; and anyway as you know, that happened, the church closed and the minister now works with the original minister in Melford, and our Mr Jeffries travels across from Eagleton. However, the Melford minister, he's about to retire, next summer, I think. And our old minister, Mr Jeffries, he will take over altogether. So, where was I? Oh well you know this yourself, after a little while the manse was sold and then we had the trouble earlier in the year with the Browning's and the terrible things that happened and the Old Manse, it's remained empty ever since but I'm led to believe that it will be going up for sale in the new year.'

'Who mentioned it going on sale, Maggie?'

'My aunty lives in Melford. She has a friend who works at Leigh's. It's all around the town.'

'I see, Maggie. Now, this may seem a silly question, but do you know anything about the heating system at the manse, for the hot water. Is it fairly new?'

'Oh, that. Seemed a bit daft to me if you don't mind me saying, Mr France. It was all fitted out with a new hot water boiler in the cellar, a new chute put in the old coal shed out the back, and all about nine or ten months before the church closed and then the manse was left empty. Can you believe it? A waste of money if you ask me.'

'I think I might agree with you there, Maggie, but just one more thing before I take my leave; I assume when all this work was done they left the cellar entrance from the manse kitchen untouched. It's still there?'

'Oh yes. They needed access from the house to the cellar and the cellar steps are still there in the kitchen. It was the coal shed steps that were altered, so they could get the coal down for the new boiler. It was all done just so it was easier for the men to drop the coal delivery.'

'Maggie, you are an asset to Moretondale and don't let anyone ever say any different.'

'You're too kind, Mr France,' she replied, 'much too kind.'

When they arrived back at Moretondale, Grainger dropped Jack France at the front of the house and then drove the car round to the garage. Jack went inside Manordale and found Mrs Hindmarsh with Mrs Whittaker in the hall. Mrs Whittaker was in some sort of *state,* her colour almost puce. Mrs Hindmarsh had a look of resigned frustration and desperation written all over her face.

'Mrs Whittaker, what is going on? I could hear your voice in the front porch. Come into the study now, please. We'll sort out whatever it is, in private.'

Suitably chastised Mrs Whittaker quietened herself down and followed Mr France. At the study door, Jack opened it and then stepped back to allow Mrs Whittaker to go through first. 'Thank you, sir. And I'm ever so sorry for my outburst just now. I really am,' Mrs Whittaker said.

'Yes. Please Mrs Whittaker, take a seat. Now I know things are a little difficult without Lily full time and Arthur incapacitated as he is, but we must all stay calm and do whatever we can to make things run smoothly. That way we can all get along and no one will end up being upset.'

'I see, sir. But I'm doing my best but it isn't really very fair at the moment. I know you are doing your best as well and it wouldn't be Manordale without you but there's too much for me to do and it coming up to a pastime and all.'

'What do you mean exactly, Mrs Whittaker?'

'I'm now expected to make up four rooms for the guests coming to stay tomorrow for the Christmas ball. Four rooms. It's bad enough with Miss Susan Packham and Miss Waterstone, but another four, that will make six rooms altogether.'

'Is that it?'

'Yes. Mrs Hindmarsh says it as if it's nothing but all she has to do is cook for them. I get all the running about to do. But there's only so much a person can take.'

'Indeed there is, Mrs Whittaker. Now, Emily prepared the first two rooms for my guests, my guests, you understand; and she will be able to help you with the preparation of the other rooms. My guests are hoping to be up and about later today, so, that's one thing you will be able to tick off your list; but Emily was the member of staff who had responsibility for their needs and wants, under my strict instruction. That was why I suggested it. I know how busy Christmas at Manordale can be. And once the rooms are ready and the Christmas ball comes it's all done by midday Christmas Eve. The guests all go home. It's a case of, 'as you were' Manordale. And it's not so bad, is it. Christmas day here? The main food is cooked the day before by Mrs Hindmarsh and this year, you're at home, and I do believe Emily and her mother are helping out here on Christmas day. No panic or raised voices needed at all.'

'No sir. Not now you put it like that.'

'Now, Mrs Whittaker, go and finish whatever it is you were doing and I believe you finish at two o'clock today, so there we are.'

'Thank you sir. I think everything's just seemed to get on top of me a little.'

'I see. But it's all sorted out now and, any problems you have, don't be shouting in this house at another member of my staff. Any problems, it is me, you come to see and I will personally sort things out, and Mrs Whittaker; before you carry on, just go down and please apologise to Mrs Hindmarsh, and then ask her if she will come up to see me in the study.'

'Right you are, sir. Thank you.'

When Mrs Hindmarsh joined Mr France in the study, she had with her Lily's notebook, and a paper list with names on it.

'Please, take a seat, Mrs Hindmarsh. I take it Mrs Whittaker apologised to you?'

'She did. It's all over and done with as far as I'm concerned. Least said, soonest mended, as they say.'

'I'm pleased to hear it. I see you have the book and what looks like a list. The guests for the $22^{nd}/23^{rd}$?'

'Yes sir.'

'Good, because that's what I wanted to talk to you about. Who's staying then on the 22nd?'

'As you no doubt know, it's just four rooms to prepare. Miss Esther Abingdon is coming up from London. She's travelling alone, so just the one room, this year. Then there's Mr and Mrs Williams coming over from Hereford. They're travelling by car and will leave early on the 24th to get back for their own celebrations. And finally, Mr Henry Wilde and his fiancée Miss Rosalind Jones. So it's about as straightforward as it gets. Four rooms. Miss Abingdon, Mr Wilde and Miss Jones are travelling from London by train and they will all require collecting from the station.'

'Have you let Grainger know the names of the guests he'll need to pick up from the station?'

'I was on my way to see him when Mrs Whittaker said to come up to see you, sir.'

'That's all right. Yes, arrange it with him. Let him have all the details. He can check when the trains will arrive, so as to be there in good time.'

'Now, any news of our other guests. Are they feeling any better?'

'Yes. And it's good news. They will lunch in the dining room.'

'Good. Anything else?'

'Yes. Sir Cecil Brookes telephoned. He asked that you call him back as soon as it was convenient.'

Jack France looked at his wristwatch. Not quite a quarter past twelve. 'I'll do it now before I go through to the dining room. Could you check please, if my guests are already there? If they are, explain that I'll join them in a few minutes. If they're not already in the dining room, there's no need to wait. Go straight across to speak with Grainger. Thank you, Mrs Hindmarsh.'

Ten Minutes Later

Jack was put through to Sir Cecil's residence in quick order and was relieved to hear that Sir Cecil was at home.

'Hello m'boy. Pleased you managed to get back to me. I expected you'd be busy and you know with me having to get away for the carol concert in Cambridge I was hoping I'd manage to catch you. And I'm pleased I have. I have news.'

'Cecil, that is music to my ears. Shall I quickly explain what I have and my thoughts, for what they're worth?'

'Fire away.'

'I'm afraid it isn't much but what I have seems to me, to be concentrated around the Old Manse. Something isn't quite right but I can't put my finger on anything. There is a hot water boiler housed in the cellar and a new coal chute in the coal shed floor. It just used to be steps to access the cellar from the garden, mainly used by workmen if needs be. The cellar can also be accessed from the kitchen in the manse, too. You see what I'm getting at here? Access through to the manse via the cellar. Anyone perhaps watching the house wouldn't see if anyone was coming or going. All the activity would be based around the back of the property.

I've had a word with Maggie Evans and she says that the new boiler for the hot water and the chute in the coal shed was all fitted out when the old minister was there, so, nothing odd on the face of it; but when I was up there a day or two ago with young Terry Franks from the village, we spotted footprints in one of the front flower beds and then when I was looking round the grounds on my own I felt sure I heard someone reciting from John's gospel, the beginning of the readings from the very new, nine lessons and carols. I would suggest that there's a distinct odour of fish, or I need a long rest.'

'I can't really suggest anything from what you've said m'boy . The footprints could be easily explained away. You've been walking in the manse grounds, well, somebody else could have as well; and not for dubious reasons, they might be interested in the property. The reciting of St. John's gospel, could it be that you might just have a lot to organise if the carol service that you're hoping for is to take place at St. Stephen's and that all the preparation that's involved could have been niggling away at you without you realising it. Playing aloud in your head. You are one of the readers, I take it?'

'Yes, I am, so that's all plausible, I suppose, but I think there could be a bigger picture about to emerge.'

'Well, what I was telephoning you about is a slightly bigger picture. Your new vicar, Reverend Smythe, you said.'

'Yes. That's right.'

'Have you seen him about the village lately?'

'A few days ago. He was at Mrs Price's cottage. She's the churchwarden for St. Stephen's. She introduced him to me.'

'And you'd not met him before? You'd not really any idea of what he would be like, or more to the point, what he looked like?

'No.'

'Now, that is fishy, then. I've heard from a Cambridge friend that Reverend Richard Smythe was due to attend the nine lessons and carols in Cambridge, as a guest, you understand. Anyway, he's suddenly not answering his calls, telephone or otherwise. Several people have tried to contact him, all to no avail. And only yesterday the local newspaper had a front-page spread asking for anyone who has knowledge of his whereabouts to get in touch with the Archdeacon in his former parish. Reverend Smythe, is missing. I'd tread carefully Jack. Don't go about rattling too many cages.'

'That's interesting. You see I spotted one or two things that made me dubious about the vicar who was sitting in Mrs Price's parlour. He was very amiable and quite likeable as a matter of fact and I thought he would be a welcome asset to the village and the parish, but then as I was leaving, I noticed his shoes, they were brown. And as I returned to Manordale I turned over some other thoughts in my mind, the letter I'd received from the diocese explicitly said that he, Reverend Smythe, hoped to call on me on the 23rd. I should have remembered the date as it's the same date as the Manordale ball, but I hadn't committed the fact to memory, and that was it. There was nothing to say in the letter that he would lead a service at St. Stephen's on the 24th; in fact it was explicit in saying that he would be coming to take over at St. Stephen's in January. I believe that whoever the man was in Mrs Price's cottage, he wasn't Reverend Richard Smythe.'

'Doesn't sound very likely, Jack, and as I said earlier, don't go rattling too many cages. I'll say my goodbyes now and, *'Watch how you go.'*

The telephone call was ended but the news that Jack had received from Sir Cecil was a gold nugget. Jack would for now, keep his own counsel but as soon as he could before the evening had cast its shadows he would call again on Mrs Price. But first however, he needed to re-read the letter that he had received informing him of the new vicar's arrival.

Jack went to his desk drawer and retrieved the letter and read through again the missive he had received only a few days ago. Mid-way through, he stopped and read the sentence again, *'... would call on him on the 23rd'*. As he had just told Sir Cecil, he couldn't think why it had slipped his mind? Of all dates, the date of the ball at Manordale should have been etched permanently in his brain.

All of this brought a whole new perspective to the problem. He now knew that there was something happening in Moretondale. It was real – not a figment of his imagination and more than that, it was imminent.

He wondered how Mrs Price might explain away the reverend she had introduced to him at her cottage, and, if he couldn't possibly be Reverend Smythe, then who was he? That was a question that needed answering.

Jack lunched with his guests and he found that they were very pleasant company, which was just what he needed. What he didn't need or want was any company on his visit to Mrs Price, but he felt duty bound as their host, to invite, Susan Packham and Miss Waterstone, to accompany him, should they wish to. He did feel though, that if there was any silver lining to be found, it was in the fact that his guests had both been incapacitated for around thirty-six hours and that their misfortune had allowed him to make his visits to the Old Manse and further afield, without any questions.

As lunch progressed to its conclusion, he decided the moment had arrived and asked them along, suggesting that while he was busy visiting with the churchwarden, that Grainger might show them the sights of Moretondale, such as they were. To Jack's relief, they politely declined. They said that they felt they would rather like to take it easy and perhaps after a game of cards; nothing too taxing, maybe, Canasta, that they would each retire to their rooms and concentrate on their costumes for the masked ball. They said that Lily had kindly furnished them with some oddments that they could use to decorate their costumes and assorted pieces of fabric.

Mrs Price's Cottage

Grainger drove the mid-grey Alvis across to Mrs Price's cottage. Jack was hoping that after his unannounced visit with Mrs Price, that he might still have time to get across to Melford and have a word with Inspector Paxton.

Grainger stayed with the car. Jack only expected to be a few minutes at the cottage.

Mrs Price opened the door of her cottage quite suddenly and Jack felt that he wasn't who she had expected to see. 'Good afternoon, Mrs Price,' he said, as he tipped his hat.

'Good afternoon, Mr France. Would you care to come in? I'm rather busy, time of the year and everything but you're more than welcome.'

'Thank you,' Jack replied and he went inside.

There were boxes all over every available space. Baubles, tinsel, and Chinese paper lanterns were awaiting their moment of glory, ready for the festive season. 'You are busy,' Jack said, 'but I promise, I won't take too much of your time. I just wondered if you'd heard anymore from the new vicar, Reverend Smythe? I haven't bumped into him at all since I first met him here and I wondered with all the organisation that has to be put in place for Christmas eve, how it was coming along. I must admit that I thought you might know as you're churchwarden.'

'It's coming along a real treat. The boys in the choir and the one or two men we have are doing a splendid job. It's marvellous to just walk in the church and hear the organ being played again. Mr Bolton is so very good.'

'Yes, I know. And your church ladies, are they doing you proud?'

'What else? The church is lovely and we have decided to just put the new Poinsettia plants around the church. They're ever so nice. Bright red and green.

Christmas colours. It'll be so much easier for us all and we can do it all quite quickly before we get ourselves ready for the ball. I am looking forward to it, to everything'

'Sounds like you've got it all in hand then, and the Poinsettia plants, I'd say they're an excellent idea. I'm sure the plants will set off St. Stephen's very well. I can't wait myself to see the finished article. Now before I forget, we've covered the church, the choir, the flowers and so on, did you say whether or not you'd seen Reverend Smythe over the last day or two?'

'No, no, I haven't seen him truth be told. Let's hope he turns up for the service, eh?' And Mrs Price forced a laugh.

Then the back door opened. 'Only me,' Jack recognised the monotone of Hubert, Mr Price.

Hubert was almost seventy years of age. More than twelve years older than Eileen Price. He was set in his ways, and as his voice was monotone he was what you might describe as monochrome in appearance. He had once had dark hair, almost jet black but this was now grey, almost to the point of white. There was nothing you could say was an interesting feature if you were to describe him. He was very much the opposite of his wife, who still had a smart appearance and who tried to retain some essence of her past youth, and yet she did at times seem older than her years. There was often a look of worry there, in her eyes. And yet the Price's always seemed quite comfortable. They appeared to have a good life together.

'He's been down the allotment,' Eileen Price said. 'I just hope he's not brought any mud in on his feet. Excuse me a moment, Mr France.' And Eileen Price went through to the kitchen. She was back in the parlour almost before she'd left. 'He's left his boots outside the back door. Thank goodness. Now, anything else?'

'Not unless you know where I should be able to find the new vicar,' Jack replied. Mrs Price simply shrugged her shoulders. There was nothing else to say to Mrs Price and Jack France left the cottage by the back door, stopping briefly to ask Hubert Price if the allotment had finally been left to sleep for the winter.

Once outside, Jack rejoined Grainger. 'Well, that didn't tell me what I needed to know, apart from the fact that Hubert Price's boots were clean. It appears that if he'd been anywhere, it wasn't near the allotment, as Mrs Price suggested, so Grainger, would you mind driving across to the Old Manse before we head into Melford?'

Grainger gave Mr France a short, sideways glance. He was sure that what Mr France had just said would make sense, eventually.

It was only a matter of minutes before the two men were alighting the car and walking around the manse grounds, as had seemed to be the custom of Jack these last few days. Jack and Grainger looked at the footprints by the porch. They were almost invisible now and there was nothing new to see. They walked the perimeter and checked the boarded over windows and doors. They looked up at the higher floors, nothing. Then they checked the coal shed. Jack pulled at the door until it was opened. Surprisingly, there had been a delivery of coal to the Old Manse. This in itself was strange. Jack and Grainger looked at each other. Jack pointed out the chute to Grainger. It was still visible. The coal was piled up against the opposite corner. This would make it easy to open the chute door and edge the coal down to the cellar below. Whoever had made the delivery of coal was familiar with the layout. There was only one coal merchant in Melford, Griggs and Sons. Jack and Grainger walked around the outside of the manse again. 'This is the point where a few days ago I heard a man's voice reciting from the bible and then saying, Amen, and suchlike. Do you hear anything Grainger?'

'No. Not a thing, sorry sir.'

'Don't apologise. The whole thing is too mysterious for words, but there is something going on. I know there is.'

The two men did three or four more laps of the manse. All was quiet but as they reached the porch at the front, Grainger put his hand out, 'Sir, listen. I hear it. I can hear it now.'

Jack stayed silent and remained where he was for only a couple of minutes. Both men heard it now,

... And the light shines in the darkness, and the darkness did not comprehend it.

'Well, what do you make of that?' Grainger said. 'There must be someone in there.'

'That is what I thought the first time I heard it. The words, they are from the book of John.'

'What do we do now, sir' Grainger asked.

'Get back to the car and drive straight to Melford. I want a word with Paxton and I intend to go to Leigh's again. Perhaps the Old Manse has been bought, after all. And if it has, I wonder by whom?'

Leigh's Land Agents and Auctioneers

Mr Leigh was out when Jack called in at the office of Leigh's land Agents in Melford. 'It's a good job my boss isn't here or else he'd have had a fit. I had to put up with him all yesterday after you'd been in the office Mr France, and he kept telling me how I 'was properly to do my job, and *'...not to give any quarter to timewasters',* and you Mr France, were mentioned by name,' the office clerk said.

'I'd best be quick, then,' Jack replied, and both he and the young woman smiled at one another. 'I apologise for not knowing your name, but we haven't been introduced.'

'It's Bernice,' the young woman replied.

'Could you possibly know Maggie Evans, who has the newsagents in Moretondale?'

'I've heard of her. I know her aunt. They are both one for chatter . . . and dare it be said, gossip.'

'The story holds water then, that's more or less what Maggie said; but I just imagined you'd be older than you are'. Bernice's face reddened; Jack didn't know whether it was anger or youth and then Bernice said. 'Stop while you're ahead Mr France and I'll take your last remark as a compliment.' 'Thank you, I did get rather carried away, but I promised to be quick and

I shall be. Do you know if there's been an offer on the manse since I enquired yesterday?'

'Yes, there has. I can't tell you who, but I believe it's to be a cash sale. Mr Leigh's over at the solicitor's office now. With Christmas fast approaching he's hoping to try and start things moving along.'

'Bernice, you've been very helpful, more than. Thank you'.

Jack took his leave and decided to call at Griggs office. It was only a short distance away and Jack told Grainger that he would walk. The car had been polished to perfection and the thought of it getting coal dust on it, didn't sit well with Jack.

Mr Griggs was no help at all to Jack. The coal hadn't come from his yard and he seemed to become rather obtuse about the whole thing as soon as he realised that whoever might be moving into the manse wouldn't be making use of his firm's coal delivery services. Jack thanked Griggs and walked back to the car. Grainger was standing by the side of it, waiting. As Jack France approached, Grainger opened the car door for him. 'I suppose I should go and have that word with Inspector Paxton, now,' Jack said.

Grainger drove the car to the police station and Jack went inside. He immediately asked for Paxton but he was told that the inspector wasn't available at the moment. 'When will he be available?' Jack asked.

'I can't really say, at the moment sir,' the desk sergeant said.

'I suppose there's no point in my waiting then?' Jack said.

'I don't suppose there is, sir,' the sergeant replied.

Jack turned and left the police station and returned to Grainger and the car.

'Grainger,' Jack said, once he had got himself settled in the car, 'would you mind driving across to the *Ring o' Bells?*'

Grainger nodded and the car set off. Jack checked his wristwatch. It was fast approaching three o' clock. 'I'd like to be there at least a couple of minutes before three,' Jack said. 'I'd like a word with George and Lucy. And there might be someone else in the bar who could be of interest.'

The Ring o' Bells

'Grainger, it's five to; come on, we might just get a drink and I'd welcome another pair of eyes and ears.'

The two men went inside. Surprised by such late customers, George Harris said, 'Mr France, Robert, you're cutting it fine.'

'What will it be, Grainger?' Jack asked.

'Just a half of bitter, please, sir.'

'Two half pints, then, thanks George. No Lucy, today?'

George spoke as he was pulling the pump to fill the half-pint glasses for his customers, 'In the back. Her brother's popped in with the Christmas cards and suchlike. They'll be talking for hours once they get started.'

Jack smiled. 'You must be pleased it's coming up to three.'

'I am and thank goodness there's no other customers in; and don't let on I was serving during drinking up time. The last thing I want is a visit from the police.'

Jack and Grainger took their drinks and went over to a table where they sat down. George called after them, 'Don't take too long over your drinks, please gents. Have a care for the landlord,' and then he smiled,

'And you know it's only a joke but as you've perhaps heard, *there's many a true word spoken in jest.'* And then George began to cover the beer pumps and remove the bar towels from the bar.

Jack acknowledged George, and then said, 'We know you too well George, that's the trouble. Any last-minute guests booked in for Christmas or will you and Lucy be taking it easy?'

George shook his head. ' Taking it easy? We hope not but no, there's no one booked in for a stay. And for the first time in a long time Lucy and myself will be at Manordale for the ball. We've decided it's best just to close on the 23rd. No offence, I hope, sir?'

'None at all,' Jack replied.

Jack and Grainger were in the pub at the most for no more than five minutes. As they left, George followed them and after they were through the door he put the catch on. They would open up again at six in the evening.

'Any thoughts, Grainger?'

'About the beer or the pub?'

'In the main about the pub. Strange to find it empty even though it was closing time. You'd have thought there'd have been a few stragglers about, but even outside, there was no one.'

'There was a chap in the car park, close to where we got out.'

'Did you notice anything about him?'

'He looked much like every other middle-aged man. A bit grey and a bit tired but other than that there was nothing to remark on.'

'Did he look smartly dressed?'

'He was tidy. He didn't look like he was dressed up to go off somewhere special.'

'Was he perhaps about to drive off as we pulled up?'

'Perhaps. He's gone now and the car's gone, so I suppose he must have been.'

'Grainger, just out of interest, do you know how long the Harris's have been at the *Ring o'Bells?* It's just that I don't remember them from my younger days in Moretondale.'

'No, I think they came here about 1912. You perhaps wouldn't remember them being so young, yourself.'

'Yes, that's probably right. So, they only moved to the area then I suppose? They're not local to Moretondale or Melford town?'

'Not that I know of. I believe they moved up here to take on the pub.'

'Thank you Grainger. That's helped a lot. A lot more than visiting the *Ring o' Bells* did. Now, if you wouldn't mind, we'll drive back to the manse.'

The Old Manse

Grainger pulled the car up on the lane a short walk away from the Old Manse. It was almost three-thirty. 'Grainger, come on,' Jack said. 'We'll leave the car here. I think we may find something of interest. I know there was no one at the pub but I had in mind a certain person might have been there. He was not. I have a feeling that our luck, however, will come in now.'

The two men walked slowly towards the manse. They looked across at Albert Riggs' cottage. They could see there was a light on inside and that the chimney was smoking. Albert must be at home. Further along the road they looked across to the other side of the road, towards Eileen Price's cottage. The curtains were drawn and the light was on. Jack and Grainger both saw the silhouettes of Mr and Mrs Price and their activities played out on the curtain. Mrs Price was being very expressive and from the actions displayed appeared to be in what might be described as an 'awful temper'. 'I wouldn't care to be on the wrong side of Mrs Price,' Grainger said. Jack agreed, at the same time wondering how Hubert Price had stood it throughout all the years they had been married; if, of course, this was a true taste of her behaviour. And then Mr France and Grainger both noticed a familiar face coming towards them. It was Mr Price; and he was carrying something.

Jack and Grainger acknowledged Mr Price and walked on. They both had the same thought; *Who had they seen in the cottage?* But neither said a word. They let Hubert Price get ahead of them and then they walked down the lane towards the manse.

At the manse they checked the usual places, the ones that they had checked before. 'Apparently,' Jack said to Grainger, 'the manse is on the point of being purchased.'

'Do you know who it might be?' Grainger asked.

'No. And I'm not entirely sure it will happen. I suspect that Mr Leigh might be in for a shock in a week's time. He wasn't in the office when I called in. Apparently he's doing his utmost to move things along. Perhaps he has his eye on a good commission if it goes through, meanwhile he's taking his eye off things that are happening closer to home.'

Grainger acknowledged Mr France. As before, he wasn't quite sure what Mr France had meant by anything that he had just said.

The manse grounds and the building looked as they ever did. The coal shed was just as it had been left. And then, as the two men came up the side of the property, Jack put his hand out. It was a signal for Grainger to be quiet and still. There was a man approaching. He was dressed in a dark overcoat and was of middle age. Jack recognised him but didn't want to speak to him at this moment in time. He rather wanted to see what he was up to. The two men drew back towards the wall of the manse, took cover as much as was possible in the evening shadows, and watched. The man didn't come to the side of the house. And all was quiet. There were no sounds or voices to be heard. Jack thought the man must be making his way to the front door. Jack and Grainger walked up the side of the house, being careful to keep in the shadows. From their position, they could see the man walk towards the coal shed and go inside. The torch he was carrying was switched on and the coal shed door was closed behind him. They waited a few minutes and then went up to the front drive of the manse, taking cover in the shrubs that lined the drive. It didn't appear that any lights inside the manse had been switched on. They stayed where they were for a few minutes and then began to walk quickly down the manse drive. As they approached the lane and turned out of the drive they could see the car ahead of them and that was when they decided to run. Within minutes they were in the car and driving as quickly as possible towards Manordale.

Once back inside the safety of the estate, Jack relaxed. He left Grainger to put the car away and once inside Manordale, Jack checked with Mrs Hindmarsh that everything was running smoothly, and then enquired about his guests. 'They seem to be having a good time sorting out their costumes for the 23$^{rd.}$. There's been a lot of laughter every time Emily's gone up to check on them, she replied.'

'That's good to hear. I have to make an important telephone call to Sir Cecil. I'll be in my study if you want me.'

Jack didn't say anything further. He went directly to his study and made his telephone call. It was just as he thought. There had been no word and no-one had heard anything from Reverend Smythe. Sir Cecil had gone on to say that the search for the missing cleric was being widened.

Jack didn't tell his thoughts to Sir Cecil. He had decided to keep his own counsel until he had spoken with Inspector Paxton. It was of the utmost importance now that Paxton listened.

Jack rang down for Grainger to bring the car round to the front of the house. He also let Mrs

Hindmarsh know that he would be out for about an hour. He was going into Melford.

Melford Police Station

Inspector Paxton was available this time and also seemed very interested in what Jack had to say and told him that he would have an officer keep a discreet eye on the Old Manse. *We have trained officers for this type of thing,* was the line that Paxton seemed to take. Jack had the distinct feeling that however many trained officers there might or might not be, there would only be Constable Waterhouse available to discreetly keep an eye on the Old Manse. And, however interested Paxton claimed to be with Jack's suggestions, he did draw the line at searching the inside of the property on what he called, *a whim*.

Jack's protestations and the fact that he had told Inspector Paxton that he had seen an unknown person, but a person he would recognise, in all probability entering the manse, just wasn't good enough, in Paxton's eyes. Paxton said that he preferred strong, hard evidence over anyone's 'gut feeling' or something that they might have seen.

Jack felt that for the moment he had done what he could and now that he had notified the police he knew that he had also done what could be construed as his *civic duty.* The affair, for the moment, was out of his hands and out of his control.

Jack returned to the car and Grainger drove them back to Manordale. Jack was quiet at first, but then as they approached the Manordale drive; Jack sat bolt upright. A thought had just occurred to him. 'Grainger, when I'm out of the car, take it and garage it and then, would you mind joining me in the study. I'd like us to have a chat.'

'I'll be about a half hour, if that's all right, sir.'

'As far as I can see, the timing will be perfect.'

At Manordale

When they were back at Manordale, Jack walked straight inside the house and through into his study. He rang for Mrs Hindmarsh, and with her usual promptness she was with him within a few minutes.

'Mrs Whittaker has left?' Jack asked.

'Yes. Three-thirty on the dot.'

'In some ways you know, she makes me laugh. And then, I tend to think, I do know where I stand with her. She's so predictable.'

'I agree with your sentiment, sir,' Mrs Hindmarsh replied.

'Now, do we have everything prepared for the guests who are arriving tomorrow, enough food and so on?'

'Everything is ready, and Emily's proving to be quite a good cook. I know that isn't how she's employed and I wouldn't take her away from any of her household duties but I often get her to help in the kitchen if she's free. And she's very good. Her mother though, is a very competent cook, Emily's inherited her mother's talents.'

'I'm pleased to hear that it's all going to plan. I didn't know that Emily had such culinary flair, though. These things are good to pick up on and thank you, Mrs Hindmarsh for letting her assist you from time to time. I've checked with Grainger and he has all the arrangements together for picking up guests from the station, so thank you for your help with that. I don't think anyone's expected to be here until after two. So, it looks as though we've everything taken care of on that front. Now, there is something else I'd like to ask, so please, Mrs Hindmarsh, take a seat.'

Mrs Hindmarsh sat down and although she was a little perplexed and wondered what on earth Mr France thought she could help with, she knew that she was ready to take on any challenge.

Jack tried to allay any fears she might have, 'Don't look so worried Mrs Hindmarsh, it's just a chat that's required and your knowledge of the village. I know that you've lived in Moretondale for a long time and you know most folk hereabouts and the comings and goings, and, most importantly, you can keep a secret. If I say anything to you it won't go any further than these four walls. And that's what I require of you. Nothing spoken of here today between us must go any further than this study. I ask that it's not even mentioned to any other members of the Manordale staff. And I think I can judge characters fairly well and I am certain that you don't belong to the *Maggie Evans* club.'

'I should hope not,' she replied. 'Anything you pass on to Maggie is around the village in less time than it takes you to walk back home.'

Jack smiled. Mrs Hindmarsh understood perfectly. He looked at Mrs Hindmarsh, and then began to speak, 'I just want to ask a couple of questions. Mrs Eileen Price, the churchwarden, she's lived in Moretondale a long time as well, hasn't she?'

'Longer than I have, sir. She was born and bred here. I only came here when I married Mr Hindmarsh, so that will be forty years next year, but I consider that to be a fairly long time.'

' Yes, I would agree. Did you know her family at all, whether she had any sisters or brothers?'

'Well, I don't know of any sisters but she did have two brothers. Like chalk and cheese they were. Ralph, he died just before my John, and then there was Richard. Now he was a bad lot. A likeable rogue I supposed you'd say. And he was handsome. A lot of the girls in the village were after Richard Smith.'

Jack broke in, 'Smith, you said. He was Richard Smith?'

'Yes. That was their name. Eileen was a Smith until she married Hubert. Poor Hubert was always very quiet, hardly would open his mouth to speak to anyone, but he was more than smitten with Eileen. I think he was just working up to ask her to marry him from the first time he saw her; and he was so much older than she was but it didn't put him off. I was actually surprised when she married him if you want to know the truth. I actually thought that Hubert Price was and would, remain a confirmed bachelor.'

'Apologies for the butting in, why did you call Hubert, poor?'

'He was always on his own. My John said that at school he was picked on, you know, by the other children. They thought he was odd, I suppose. You see he was very quiet, studious was what John said he was like, always had his nose in a book; didn't much want to be out with the lads.'

'I see. I can appreciate that, and I know Hubert was quiet. Whenever I bumped into him here or in Melford it was all he could do most times to say, '*Hello*' or '*Good Morning*'. Please, carry on Mrs Hindmarsh.'

'Where was I? Oh yes, Richard. What was there not to like? Handsome he was, and he could as they say, *charm the birds off the trees,* but he never really had a steady job, he was always trying to get one over on people, even those he knew, his family and friends. He ended up in trouble with the police as a young man and he might still be, for all I know. I haven't heard anything of him for years or seen him; and Eileen, she never mentions him at all.'

'Were they close, the family? But I suppose the one I want to know more about is Richard?'

'I suppose they were. My John and Ralph were quite friendly but John never mentioned Richard too much. I think that by the time I'd married John, the Smith family had had quite enough of Richard and his goings on. Ralph married after me and John and then he moved into Melford, that's where his wife Grace was from, and then after that John only used to see him occasionally on market day; they'd perhaps go over to the Three Nuns on the marketplace. I told you Richard was in trouble with the police and so on, well it was only a matter of time before he ended up being sent to prison for theft, and then, well that was the time when Ralph severed all ties with Richard; in fact the family were none too pleased at what he'd done and tried to distance their selves from him and his criminal activities. They said he was a disgrace to the family and that was that, but with Eileen, it was different. She was six or seven years younger than the boys. Ralph was the eldest of the three, then Richard and then Eileen, and she was very close to Richard. It broke her heart when he left the village but after a stint in prison there was no way he could come back to Moretondale. Not really.'

'And if he was to come back to Moretondale, do you think you might be able to recognise him? I know it has been a long time.'

'I don't know, truth be told; and it has been a long time since I ever saw him. I can tell you that when he was young he was very dark though, his hair almost like jet and I suppose across the eyes he was a lot like Eileen. Yes, they both had dark brown eyes.'

'You've been a great help, Mrs Hindmarsh.'

There was a knock on the study door. 'Yes, come through, please,' Jack said. And the door opened and Grainger stepped inside. 'The car's away now, Mr France, so I thought I'd best come straight up, as you asked.'

'That's fine, Grainger. Take a seat.'

Grainger sat down by the window while Jack and Mrs Hindmarsh drew their conversation to a close.

When Mrs Hindmarsh had left, Grainger stood up and took the recently vacated chair.

'Thanks Grainger, for coming in for this chat. It's about everything that's going on at the manse. I've spoken to Inspector Paxton about the things that seem to be going on there and voiced some of my suspicions but you know what he's like. He's assigned a constable to keep a discreet eye on the property. Pound to a penny that will be Constable Waterhouse and his bicycle.'

'Are we …, pardon me, sir, is it all right to ask, do you think someone is perhaps trapped inside the manse?'

'I do, but I don't think they're in any danger. In fact, I think they will probably be being looked after very well. But I think there's more going to happen. And I think that whatever the 'more' is, will happen at the Manordale Ball on the 23rd. And Grainger, I might require your assistance if I am correct in my thinking.'

December 22nd

The morning was passed in preparation for the arrival of the guests to Manordale for the ball.

Jack called in at the Graves' cottage to check up on Arthur. He wondered whether or not Arthur would feel like taking part in the festivities, but there was no need for the question to be asked. As soon as Lily opened the door and Arthur saw who the visitor was he said,

'I'm looking forward to tomorrow at the hall, Mr France.'

'Then, as I said, I shall personally come and do the honours regards getting you across to Manordale. And you Lily, everything prepared?'

'Yes. I'm just so pleased we can make it, after all.'

'We'll arrange for you to be out of the huddle of people, Arthur,' Jack said. And then Jack handed to Arthur a small box he had brought into the cottage with him. 'This is for you. I know you are a lover of chocolate, so I picked up some novelties from Maggie's. There should be enough for a day or two.'

'Thank you very much, sir', Arthur said.

Lily looked at her husband, and then at the box, 'Perhaps we might share,' she said, laughing.

Jack looked at them both and smiled. 'I'll be on my way shortly, but before I do I'll update you on things at Manordale. Mrs Hindmarsh is doing a splendid job in your absence Lily, and Emily, we are finding out also is quite a good cook; and I'm pleased to report that our other invalids are now out and about. Miss Susan Packham and Miss Waterstone were able to dine with me last night and we had breakfast together this morning. They both of course, will be at the ball tomorrow and later today Grainger will pick up those who are travelling down by train. Oh, almost slipped my mind and this is rather important; Lily, can you remember, or help me to remember, which of the ladies always attends the ball in those fancy get ups that she tops off with a diamond tiara and usually a pearl brooch that she claims are paste and only worth a trifle, but that we know perfectly well are the real thing. Is it Lady Dennistoun Hardie or Lady Percival?'

Later That Day

Miss Packham and Miss Waterstone were in the sitting room at Manordale. Jack joined them just before two o'clock. Grainger had just left to pick up the first guests from the station. Miss Esther Abingdon, Mr Henry Wilde and his fiancée, Miss Rosalind Jones were all travelling by train and would now arrive at Manordale within the hour.

'Good afternoon, ladies. I'm afraid I've not been the most attentive of hosts over the last day or two, but it should all be plain sailing from now on,' Jack said, as he walked into the sitting room and sat down in one of the easy chairs. His guests both looked up. Susan Packham said that it couldn't be helped and that it was perfectly understood, and that they themselves hadn't really needed a host, just to feel better and what a bother they must have been adding extra work for the already busy staff. Jack smiled, 'Don't apologise, I'm only too pleased that you're both up and about again. It would have been awful if your malady had carried on into Christmas and upset your celebrations. Even when you're away from home you want this time of the year to be special'

'Jack, as you say, there's no need for apologies. It's all done,' Susan Packham said.

Jack continued. 'Understood, but Estate business can be rather tiresome at times and I feel that I haven't done as much as I really should to be prepared, myself. Still, that's an end to it. Let's move on to more pleasant conversation. Tomorrow is where I take on the role of looking after my staff for the evening and of course all the village are invited, should they care to come along.'

'You do have some help though?' Susan asked.

Jack laughed. 'Yes. The running of the event without any help would be far too much. I have hired staff coming in tomorrow afternoon, caterers and so on. They'll arrive after lunch. And you know it's a costume ball. Have you thought up any ideas? You need to have costumes at the ready.'

'I have,' Susan replied, 'and I know it has to be kept secret, so my lips are sealed. But we might do a costume share. That's what we were thinking of.'

'Sounds intriguing,' Jack said.

'More silly than intriguing,' Susan said.

Jack stood up and moved across to the window. 'I've arranged for Mrs Hindmarsh to bring up afternoon tea for us as soon as the first guests arrive. I thought it would be a good way for you all to get to know one another. I hope you won't mind.'

'Do you know?' Susan replied. 'I rather think I like Christmas in the country.'

By a little after three-fifteen in the afternoon, the three guests had been brought from the station and were safely ensconced at Manordale. At three-thirty, afternoon tea was served in the sitting room and the guests all began to get to know one another. Mr Henry Wilde, a long-time friend of Jack's, introduced Rosalind, his new fiancée.

'I must say,' Jack said, 'you've kept all this a secret, but how?'

'Stealth,' he said, smiling, and everyone laughed.

The time passed quickly and pleasantly in light conversation but there was no sign of the Williams's. It wasn't like them to do a 'no show'. Jack hoped that they hadn't had a problem with the car.

Susan Packham got up and went over to the young couple who were very *close* with each other. 'Congratulations, both of you, a very exciting time ahead. All the planning to get things just right. I expect you will be very busy indeed in the new year,' she said, and then went back to where she'd been sitting. Miss Waterstone remained seated and observed. Her eyes for a moment caught those of the young couple. It momentarily unnerved Henry who almost at once put his arm around Rosalind's waist and pulled her close and they both smiled at each other, each holding the others gaze for a long moment. Minutes later Jack heard the telephone in the hall and excused himself from his guests while he left to answer it, explaining as he went about Arthur's misfortune as the reason he was answering his own telephone.

'Manordale, Mr Jack France speaking. Oh, hello you. What's the game? I was expecting you here at any time. . . You can't make it?. . . No. Of course I understand. That's too bad. We've a few folk staying at Manordale over Christmas, and I was looking forward to meeting up. It seems an age since we last got together and you've not been in London when I've been down.' There was a pause before Jack continued, 'I know George and I understand. But as soon as you and Effie get a chance you have to make a space in your diary to come over to Manordale and stay here for a few days. I have your word? I'll hold you to that old man. Happy Christmas to you, too. 'Bye.'

Jack replaced the telephone and rejoined his guests in the sitting room.

'I'm afraid some friends of mine from Hereford are unable to join us, so, it would appear, the gang's all here, as they say.'

'Is there a running order for tomorrow evening? I know we have to keep our costumes a secret on pain of death from my attendance at previous Manordale Balls, but I don't want to miss a thing,' Esther said.

'As long as we're all in the ballroom for seven forty-five or thereabouts, everything will go to plan. The band will be primed, and at nine o' clock the buffet food will be served in the small room off the hallway. There will be staff around to assist, so no one has anything to worry about,' Jack replied.

'Dare we ask who the band is this year?' Henry asked.

'You may, but I'm not telling you a thing. That's part of the Manordale surprise.'

December 23rd

The day dawned cool and frosty but it wasn't so bright. Jack knew that today was the day he would have to remain focused on everything the day brought to him, for good or bad, whatever it might be; particularly at the ball tonight. He decided that after breakfast he would walk up towards the Old Manse and see if Constable Waterhouse was anywhere in sight.

Jack spotted the bicycle first – no sign of Waterhouse. Jack walked a little farther on along the road and then stopped, taking cover by the side of a tree. After a few minutes more he saw Constable Waterhouse walk out of the drive of the manse and walk across to his bicycle.

He took some bicycle clips from the breast pocket of his jacket, replaced them around his trousers and then cycled off in the direction of Maggie Evans' shop. Jack thought he was probably going to stock up on supplies to relieve the boredom of watching nothing happen. Jack, satisfied that all that could apparently be done, was being done, turned and walked back to Manordale. Once inside, Jack went and checked in with Mrs Hindmarsh and Mrs Whittaker. Together, they had everything under control and young Emily was keen to say how much she was looking forward to the ball.

Jack really did know when things were good, and at Manordale that seemed to be the case more often than not. He was content and a man happy with his lot.

Jack then called in at the garage to have a quick word with Grainger. He wanted to check that all was ready for the evening and Grainger knew exactly what was expected of him. After that he called in at the Graves' cottage. Lily and Arthur were looking forward to the evening and Jack agreed that he would be over at the cottage again for a quarter past seven, in order to take charge of the wheelchair duties.

On his return walk to Manordale, Jack bumped into some of his guests; Esther was walking in the garden with Susan Packham and Miss Waterstone.

'It's not a bad morning, though I do hope the sun manages to break through or by late afternoon it will appear that it's been dark all day,' Jack said.

Heads nodded in agreement. 'It doesn't matter to us,' Esther said, 'just being in the country air after the smog of London is a real treat.' Susan Packham and Miss Waterstone agreed.

Jack left them to their walk and went off to have a word with Riley who was attending to some lights on the fir tree in the grounds. 'Will you make sure we have lighting set up in the usual place, and ready for the cars to park this evening?' Jack said.

'Mr France, I'm on to it already.'

'Good. Thanks Riley, and when that's done, you may as well get off home and then in whatever guise you choose, hopefully you will be at Manordale later.'

'Thank you sir. Yes, I'll be there.'

Jack nodded and walked briefly around the grounds, wondering if he would catch his guests again. He didn't. It appeared that they must have decided to go back inside Manordale. He turned and went into the house. Once through the doors he sighed and then straightened himself up, held his shoulders back and taut for a second or two, before relaxing again. It was funny how moods could change in a few minutes. Jack suddenly felt as though he shouldn't be the best company at the moment and ignoring the chat coming from the sitting room, he went into his study and rang for a pot of tea to be brought up.

That Afternoon

Emily brought the tea up to the study and placed the tray on the table to the side of the desk where Jack was seated. 'Thank you, Emily. I was rather hoping Mrs Hindmarsh would have been the deliverer of rations but I expect she's rather busy.'

'Yes sir. The telephone began ringing non-stop almost as soon as you'd left the house. Mrs Hindmarsh stayed in the hall for a few minutes just to take the calls. She had been up and down a couple of times and just missed the caller, so she decided she'd best stay where she was and see if anyone telephoned back, which they did. It was a bit of a to do, I can tell you, what with the staff and the caterers just telephoning to check the arrangements.'

'But that had all been settled. Do you know whether it was a gentleman or a lady who telephoned?' Jack asked.

'I don't know sir. I know Mrs Hindmarsh was getting a bit flustered, though.'

'Thanks Emily. That's very useful, and if you would ask Mrs Hindmarsh to come up to the study, please, and if the telephone rings and you're on your own, ignore it. Mrs Hindmarsh will be but a few minutes.'

Emily left the study and returned to the kitchen. She passed the message on to Mrs Hindmarsh, and then added, 'But he's a bit strange, or so it seems to me, Mr France. Watch out in case he turns.'

'Turns into what? A pumpkin? You read too many books my girl. Now you carry on with what you were doing and I'll go and see Mr France.'

In the study Jack had already telephoned the hired staff, and it was as he thought, no one from the firm had telephoned Manordale. He was on the telephone to the caterers when there was a knock at the door and Mrs Hindmarsh entered. Jack gestured for her to take a seat. 'I see. So it wasn't you then? That's all right. I just wanted to check and as arranged; we'll see you later this afternoon. Thank you, good day.' Jack replaced the receiver. 'Emily mentioned the telephone calls you'd had. A good thing she did. Neither were from who they professed to be. Hoax calls. Did you give any details about guests?'

'Not in so many words. It was the caterer, or someone who said they were the caterers, a lady, she asked if there was anyone from the village attending. She'd lived in Moretondale as a young girl and thought she might remember some names.'

'Did you mention anyone by name?'

'Yes and no. I didn't mention names until she said isn't there a family by the name of Dennistoun Hardie in Moretondale? I said yes and then she said, and a family named Prin, and I thought she must mean Percival and told her the name. That was all.'

'Did she mention the Ball?'

'Only in as much as she said, '*It would be fun to see them this evening.*' I told her that it was a costume ball, so she might not recognise anybody. She laughed at that and the telephone was put down.'

'Did you recognise the voice?'

'No. But whoever it was, I could tell they were local.'

'And the hired staff, they are coming as usual from Teale's in Melford. I personally sorted out everything out with them. Did they ask anything in particular, Mrs Hindmarsh?

'No. To be honest I think I didn't quite take it all in. I'm sorry, Mr France. I feel I've let you and Manordale down.'

'No. No, you could never do that. It was my fault for not getting someone in to cover for Arthur but I thought we might manage. I've learnt something from this, Mrs Hindmarsh and if it's anyone's fault, it is mine. Now don't you worry over anything. You've done nothing wrong.'

When Mrs Hindmarsh had left the study Jack drank his tea. The solitude and quiet gave him the time to sit and consider his thoughts and the things he knew. In the quiet of the study it seemed as if all the pieces in this Christmas jigsaw were finally coming together. He thought he knew the who and the where of the puzzle. The what, he was pretty certain about. The how, likewise; and the when would be tonight at the Manordale Ball; more or less any time between eight o'clock and midnight. Jack smiled. He had his plans set in place. Later, he would visit Inspector Paxton and see if he could make him change his mind about acting on anything other than concrete evidence.

Lunch was eaten slightly earlier than usual so that Mrs Hindmarsh could leave the way clear for the arrival of the hired staff and caterers.

Mrs Hindmarsh had calmed down somewhat and was back to her usual self, although she still felt she had been taken for a ride by persons unknown and that rather annoyed her. If only she knew who was responsible, she'd let them have the sharp side of her tongue.

Much to the contrary of Jack's first thoughts, lunch was a pleasant affair and Jack was pleased that his mood had brightened. The conversation was light, and Jack was pleased that everyone got on so well together. It would make it all a lot easier tonight. He was also pleased with the band that he had lined up for the evening's entertainment. He was certain it would make a few jaws drop. Another part of the evening's events was that a cocktail waiter, Marcel, would be on hand. Jack had a spot in mind in the hall where there would be a black and chrome counter to imitate a bar and glass backed shelves to be filled with bottles, glasses, and shakers. Jack also had a couple of stands for ice buckets. He would assemble all that later when the house guests were busy.

Henry and Rosalind had decided that they should take a trip into Melford to get costumes for the ball. They had each decided that for them, hiring was possibly the safest bet. Esther said that she and Susan and Miss Waterstone had decided to help each other. Susan said that the idea was a hoot and it would knock spots off any other costumes, and then crossed her fingers in a jokey gesture. Jack said that it wasn't to be taken too seriously at all, by anyone and that it definitely wasn't a competition; but he did, however, wish them all well. When the conversation had reached a natural conclusion, Jack made his apologies to his guests and added, that as they were all busy, he would attend to estate business for the next hour or so and them join them again briefly, before the ball. It was important, he said, that he didn't know the identities of any of them. It all added to the fun.

Jack returned to his study and telephoned Melford police station and asked to be put through to Inspector Paxton. He waited a few minutes and then heard the tones of Paxton on the other end of the line.

'Inspector, thank you for taking my call. I know you're busy and the season of goodwill and everything is almost upon us, but the Old Manse, that's why I'm telephoning. I think you should perhaps listen to . . .'

'Mr France, I've listened to your ramblings, and if you don't mind me saying so, I have taken things seriously. Perhaps too seriously when there isn't really anything other than your word to go on, and in response to this I've put a man discreetly observing the manse…,'

'I know. I've seen Constable Waterhouse.'

'Do not interrupt me, please, Mr France. And I do know what you're saying but I cannot search a property on a whim. If there's someone in there why aren't they making more of a fuss, eh? And why has no one reported a missing person to me at the station? Had you thought of that?'

'I had, Inspector, and as I mentioned, there is notice of . . .'

'Mr France, I have heard all this before. I do not propose to go raking over old coals with you. Now have you anything new to add?'

'Yes. I have. Tonight, it's the Manordale Ball, and I'm expecting . . .'

'And I'm sure you and your guests will all have a lovely time. Good-day Mr France, and Happy Christmas!'

Jack replaced the receiver, determined not to let Paxton deflate his spirit. Paxton really was the bottom of the barrel, at times. Jack left the house and went outside. Riley was still making good the lights for the car parking area. 'Nearly done there, have you?' Jack asked.

'Just about sir. And then I'm off to get ready for tonight. Muriel's really looking forward to the ball, but then she always does.'

Jack left Riley to his work and went back into the house. He asked that Emily should wait in the hall until he returned, to take any telephone calls there might be and then he put on his overcoat and hat. He checked his coat pocket for a pipe, there was one there and a ready supply of matches. He set off, pipe in hand, in direction of the Old Manse.

It was only a few minutes' walk and it was quite pleasant. The morning had been white with frost, but that had more or less cleared and a watery sun was peeping through the clouds. Jack thought to himself there was some light to the day, after all.

On the lane up to the manse there was no sign of Waterhouse or his bicycle. Jack walked past the manse to see if there was any sign of life in the manse grounds. There was not. Mrs Price's cottage was only across the road. Jack walked across the road but could see that it was all in darkness. He didn't bother going any closer to check but walked on to Albert Riggs' cottage. Albert was at home.

'I wondered if you'd noticed Constable Waterhouse on the lane?' Jack asked.

'He was there this morning but he wasn't there after lunch. I always check the lane after lunch, just to see what's what. There was no sign of Constable Waterhouse, that's for certain.'

'Thanks Albert, and will you be at Manordale tonight?'

'There's nothing that will stop me, sir.'

Jack walked back to Manordale. So, this is what Inspector Paxton calls 'discreet'. He shook his head as he walked, disgusted at the incompetence of the local Inspector.

'Where's Emily?' Jack asked as he entered the hall and saw Mrs Hindmarsh in front of him. 'Emily's down in the kitchen, at my request. I said that if she found Mrs

Whittaker they might both go as soon as they'd finished any work they had to do and get off home to get ready for tonight. Anyway, then this little lot arrived,' Mrs Hindmarsh gestured towards packages of various shapes that took up most of the hall. 'So, I said to Emily that instead of her going quite so soon that we should swap places for a while; and thank goodness you've arrived back home is all I can say, Mr France.'

Mrs Hindmarsh was quite surrounded by boxes of all shapes and sizes. 'It's all right, Mrs Hindmarsh. I knew that this was due. I should've mentioned it. I must say though, there's more of it than I expected; it's all part of my staging for tonight.'

'I'm pleased you know what it's for, sir,' Mrs Hindmarsh replied. Jack smiled.

'Have there been any other calls for me?'

'Yes, I suppose. Not calls but *other*, that's what I'd call it. The caterers have arrived and they're now busy in the kitchen. When the waiting staff arrive, I'll take my leave, and then let Emily go, shall I?'

'You could get along now too, if you like. I'll manage now. And the waiting staff shouldn't be too much longer. Oh, and don't forget Mrs Whittaker,' Jack said, 'or has she already left?'

'There's no forgetting Mrs Whittaker, and yes, I thought it best to let her go,' Mrs Hindmarsh replied.

Jack took the boxes and organised them as he saw fit, according to the labels attached to each. He would start the proper setting out of them, later, with help from some of the staff who were due to arrive.

He left Mrs Hindmarsh to deal with Emily and said that he was going to check on the Graves'. He shouldn't be too long.

Jack knocked at the cottage door. Lily answered. 'Oh, Mr France, do come in.'

Jack walked through to the sitting room and took a seat close to where Arthur was. 'How is it going, Arthur?'

'All right. I just keep reminding myself what a silly thing it was to do and I'll be so pleased when the plaster is removed and I can be out and about again around Manordale. I find it hard to believe that I really did this.'

'Don't rush it. When you're someone who's used to being busy it must come as a complete shock to have to sit and do nothing, but these things take time, and you might like to know this, and I have it on good authority, that when a break is nearly better it starts to itch. A knitting needle is a good thing to use to get down the plaster to attend to the itchy place - as long as you don't scratch too hard. So, wait for the itch signal, Arthur.'

Lily looked aghast. 'Oh no Mr France. I'll not have that. Arthur will have to put up with the itch, I'm afraid. I don't want to have to be going up to the hospital with Arthur and asking them to retrieve a lost knitting needle.'

Jack looked at Lily, 'Sorry to have mentioned it, Lily. Just ignore my attempt at advice, but the thing I've come over to see you about, is tonight. I won't see you again now until I come over later to take you across to the house for the ball. Everything's coming together well, I'm relieved to say, and Riley has done a spectacular job with the lights. So, remember what I asked you to bring with you. It could be important.'

'It's here sir. All ready.' Arthur reached down and held up his walking stick.

Before The Ball

Jack returned to Manordale and the preparation was all going to plan. The staff had arrived to take over and were under the watchful eye of their manager, a Mr Longfellow.

Emily had left Manordale but Mrs Hindmarsh was still bustling and flustering in the hall and Jack decided more force was required so he resorted to gently and calmly ushering her from the building.

A space was then cleared and the bar and the seating area were set up in the hall. All that was needed now was the cocktail waiter; and he would arrive by seven o'clock.

Jack France thanked the staff for all their help and then told them where they should be required to assist later in the evening. He then took their leave and went downstairs to check on the caterers and show the catering manager, Mr Jarvis, where the food was required. It would be a hot buffet, after the band had played their first set. There were chairs where guests could 'rest' for a few minutes while eating. Jack had also requested some nibbles to be set out in the dining room on the sideboard so that his 'at home' guests could have something to eat before everything was under way. That was to be served no later than five o'clock and he wanted everything cleared by six. So far so good. He checked his wristwatch, four-thirty p.m..

Back upstairs, Jack caught up quickly with his guests and gave them all the arrangements for the light food that was to be served in the dining room before the ball.

All were back at Manordale apart from Henry and Rosalind. Jack wasn't too concerned but thought it odd that they hadn't returned as they had only gone into Melford to track down costumes for tonight's ball.

Jack went into his study and poured himself a whisky, sat back in the chair by his desk and relaxed. He would join his guests in the dining room, later.

At exactly five o'clock by the chimes of the church clock, Jack got up from his chair and went into the dining room. It was all set up as he had requested and there were four staff to serve food and two to serve tea or coffee. Everyone who should have been there, was present; but only if you didn't count Henry and Rosalind. Still very obvious by their absence.

Jack chatted with his guests and asked if anyone had seen anything of Henry and Rosalind but no one had, not since earlier in the day. Miss Waterstone mentioned that they seemed pretty thick earlier, and that she was also surprised that no one else had noticed anything. But it wasn't really her place to say anything and Miss Waterstone said that she would only speak on it, if asked. Susan Packham told Miss Waterstone to be quiet, there wasn't any need for gossip, and that's what it was turning into; and if there was anything at all to be said then she would do it. Jack smiled, but all the same he was a little concerned and the way Susan Packham and Miss Waterstone were going on, he was also becoming a little confused.

Jack reminded them of the time for the ball and said that from now on he would be busy, but if anyone needed to speak to him at all, they could. They would easily recognise him as he wouldn't be in costume. He went upstairs to get ready for the evening. His dinner suit was already laid out. He started filling the bath and began to prepare everything else he needed while the bath filled. At twenty-past six, he was suitably attired and sitting in the entrance hall of Manordale. He had staff ready to take coats and wraps and he was only waiting now for the cocktail waiter and the band. At half-past six he would walk over to the Graves' cottage.

As the chimes struck the half hour, Jack left for the cottage. He mentioned to one of the cloakroom girls that he would only be gone for ten or fifteen minutes and that if there were any messages, telephone or otherwise, would she take them? She said that she would.

At five to seven, Jack was back inside Manordale with Lily and Arthur Graves. He pushed the wheelchair through to the ballroom and made sure Arthur and Lily were comfortable before he left them to go back to the entrance hall. As soon as he was seated by the entrance the young girl he had given the message to came over to him, 'Oh, excuse me Mr France, there was a telephone call while you were away. It was from Henry and Rosalind. Henry said to let you know they'd taken the afternoon train and were on their way to Gretna Green. They said thanks for your hospitality and they hoped to catch you on their return. They didn't want to leave you in the lurch but it was the only way they could do things.'

Jack thanked the girl and then sat down and set off laughing. *Henry the old rogue. Using the Manordale Ball for his own ends. Miss Waterstone had apparently been right.*

7.45p.m. Manordale

The cocktail waiter was now in his position at the newly assembled cocktail bar. He introduced himself as *Marcel,* although Jack doubted somewhat the authenticity of his French accent.

The band had also arrived and were setting up in the ballroom. How the dancing would go, Jack hadn't really thought. The older generation of Moretondale might think it a little odd but he was absolutely sure that everyone would enjoy it; even when the expected incident happened at the ball, as he knew it would, Jack was sure that he could pull everything off, successfully.

Earlier in the afternoon, after his conversation with Paxton, Jack had had another telephone conversation with Inspector Grant at Scotland Yard. Inspector Grant didn't think that Jack was rambling at all. He had taken everything Jack had said as highly significant.

Jack was now getting ready for the influx of guests and also watching out for two in particular; the innocent party and the guilty party. He knew that even with their costumes and masks he would spot them, easily.

The guests collected their masks at the porch, as per instructions and filtered through to the ballroom. The band were behind a screen of sorts and the odd musical noise was heard although nothing was being played as yet. The talk was of 'who it could be' and suggestions were being proffered although none of the suggestions that Jack had heard, was correct.

Marcel was busy shaking cocktails. The staff would then take the trays through to the ballroom.

Jack had asked that the first cocktails taken through to the ballroom should be Gimlets, Martinis and Coconut Champagne Punch, after that, the guests were on their own. Jack's own favourite was a Dry Martini cocktail garnished with a green olive; and when most of the guests had arrived that was the time when Jack would leave the staff on the door to attend to any latecomers, and he would collect a Martini from the bar and then, with glass in hand, Jack would go into the ballroom to welcome everyone to the Manordale Ball, 1928, and then the band would play.

7.55 p.m.

Jack knew that the guilty party had arrived at the ball. He welcomed him as he had done all his guests, and exchanged pleasantries with him before the guest made his way through into the ballroom. A moment or two later Jack beckoned a young waitress over to him. 'I need you to take this note to a gentleman waiting in the car parking area. He will be standing outside his car and he will be wearing a dark brown overcoat and a trilby hat. All you need to do is to give him this note and say that Jack France sent you from the house. There won't be a reply given. As soon as the note is delivered you can return to the house.'

     The young waitress took the note from Jack and then he passed her a torch. 'Take this, you might need it,' he said. And then Jack watched her as she left the house before he returned to his position in the hall. By the time she returned it was two minutes past eight. She handed the torch back to Jack and then returned to her position in the hall. At five past eight Jack stood up, took a Martini from the bar, made sure that the staff manager, Mr Longfellow left someone in authority at the door, as it would be soon time for him to go through to the ballroom and officially welcome the guests. Jack also mentioned that it was unlikely that anyone else would turn up, although he knew that the victim was not yet within the confines of Manordale, but that information was something that for the moment he could keep to himself. Jack told Mr Longfellow that whether or not any more guests arrived that there must be someone at the door throughout the evening. Mr Longfellow said that he thought it best to take on that responsibility himself.

Before entering the ballroom, Jack turned to take one last look at the hall. He then breathed a sigh of relief when a couple walked through the hall door of Manordale. He watched as Mr Longfellow greeted them. Jack smiled to himself. He recognised at once the diamond tiara that the lady was wearing and also the pearl brooch that was on her dress. She was dressed as Marie Antoinette, of that there was no mistake and her partner was dressed as Louis XVI. Sir John Percival and his wife Lady Mary made a handsome couple.

In The Ballroom

There was uproarious laughter in the ballroom as Jack entered. He didn't think he could be responsible for such laughter and as he looked to the centre of the room, he at once saw why the guests were all laughing. He recognised the grey costumes and he had noticed one person dressed in a glittery top trimmed with gold and silver stars and wearing baggy, gold lame trousers when the particular three persons in question had all entered the hall, quite independently of each other. It could only be Miss Esther Abingdon, Susan Packham and Miss Waterstone. The three people who were working together on something silly. Their costume was now unveiled as an elephant and its mahout. He wondered how long whoever was the rider, would remain atop the elephant, and whether elephant or the rider would tire first, but he thought he had a good idea.

Jack walked on to the centre of the ballroom and raised his glass to all who were there, saying that in Moretondale the official start of Christmas was always the Manordale ball; he then went on to give a short speech after which he said that the band would play and for those who danced, the dancing might begin.

Speech and formalities finished, Jack walked towards the curtained off area that was concealing the band and their identity from the guests. Jack then poked his head through the curtain and could be heard speaking with the band. He then turned to face the guests waiting on the ballroom floor, and then he spoke in an animated fashion, 'Ladies and Gentlemen, the band are ready, are you?'

There was a lot of laughter and cries of 'YES', filled the room.'

'Good,' Jack said, 'because before the band begin their set tonight, they're going to play one for us under wraps. My question is, will anyone recognise the band when they're not in plain sight. Perhaps. Right, take it away Maestro.'

At Jack's word, the band struck up. To those in the know it was easily recognisable as *'Take Your Finger Out Of Your Mouth (I Want To Kiss You)'* 'Any takers?' Jack asked. There were none. 'Right the curtain is moving apart, this is where all is revealed. Let's see if we have anyone recognise them now?'

The mahout called out from the top of the elephant. 'It's Ambrose! Ambrose and his band. Mr France, how did you manage that? They play at the May Fair.'

'I do have friends in London, you know,' Jack said, a cheeky grin on his face, 'and by the way, the cocktail waiter for the evening, Marcel at the bar, he's from there as well; and he certainly knows how to mix his cocktails. Everyone, please do enjoy the Manordale festivities; and for your information, the Supper Buffet will be served at quarter to nine, and afterwards, more from Ambrose and his band.'

At this announcement there were more cheers and applause from the guests. And all the while, Jack was watching the King and Queen of France and a mediaeval pedlar who was wearing brown shoes. His accomplice could be any one of the women who were at the ball. Jack knew who she was, he had worked that out but he couldn't say who or where she was at the moment when all those in front of him were wearing masks.

Jack went over to Arthur and Lily Graves. They were watching closely the dancers on the ballroom floor. They spoke briefly to say that they hadn't noticed anyone do anything out of the ordinary, but they would keep watching. Jack said, 'I don't think anything will happen before the food has been served. I think it will be afterwards when the guests take to the floor again; we'll just have to be patient, but in all of this, don't let the French aristocracy out of your sight.'

Jack then went out to the bar and ordered another Martini. Then he went out to the front of Manordale and took in what he could of the landscape. Even with lights for parking, the trees overshadowed everything. It was still difficult to see other than outlines in the near distance and further away, nigh on impossible to see anything at all.

He began to think about the ones in the Old Manse. The ones being held against their will. Did they have any idea that their hour of salvation was imminent?

Jack could picture the inside of the manse from the last time he had been inside although it was now a few months ago, when the Brownings were there and then everything that came from that. He knew that Constable Waterhouse and Reverend Smythe would be quite comfortable. All the furnishings of the house were left inside when the property was vacated. The only things to be removed were personal effects and documents. The house, when the Browning's bought it, had been bought furnished, and so these items remained. Even if, and it was possible, that reverend Smythe and Constable Waterhouse were locked in one of the rooms, they would have everything they needed to hand. And though there may be another person, at this moment unknown, watching them for most of the time, Jack felt that Richard Smith had no reason to do them harm, so whoever the unknown person was, must also be of that inclination. It was just that at this moment Jack wanted Reverend Richard Smythe and Constable Waterhouse safely out of the Old Manse. That would be the only way to bring this affair to an end, when the captives were freed and safe again.

Mr Richard Smith was a rogue whose money went through his fingers like water from a tap. Theft was his occupation; when he wasn't otherwise detained for his crimes.

For a few minutes Jack considered how people made their life choices. Some were not really bad people; they simply made the wrong choices. A lot of them were intelligent and planned things to the 'nth detail, but there was always, at some point in their *careers,* the one tiny mistake that gave everything away. The slip that told you *who* the person was. Jack took another sip of his Martini and went back into Manordale and into the ballroom to speak with Grainger.

As pre-arranged; Grainger was in costume as a country yokel, complete with corn ears stuffed down his gaiters. Grainger was directly opposite where the Graves' were seated. He would wait for any sign of disturbance amongst the guests and go straight into action. Jack had advised Grainger of the several possibilities and of the lines of action to take in each case.

Everyone was enjoying themselves and the band played on. A member of the catering staff came over to Jack, 'Excuse me, Mr France; the buffet is being prepared to be served and the staff are waiting. When the guests are ready they can make their way through.'

'Thank you. I'll let them know.' Jack walked over to where the band were playing and had a word with Ambrose. It was decided there would be a short number played and then the band and the guests would take a welcome break.

Jack knew that it would be when the guests returned to the ballroom that an 'incident' would take place.

While the guests were enjoying a break, the Graves', and Grainger, stayed together in the ballroom. Grainger brought them all some food through and Jack assigned a member of the waiting staff to bring them drinks; and then Jack returned to the room where the buffet was being served and studied his guests intently. There was one person missing and he hadn't yet worked out their 'costumed' identity. He was hoping this wouldn't cause a problem. Watching as the guests enjoyed the food he saw that the mahout had now stepped down from the elephant. He expected it would be a relief for all concerned.

Over at the manse, Reverend Smythe and Constable Waterhouse were being watched over by Mr Hubert Price. Jack was correct. They were in no danger of any serious harm but Mr Price had waved a gun around a couple of times adding a touch of bravado to the proceedings and to give the impression that he meant business. Neither of the men knew him. Only one of them was a resident of Moretondale and Constable Waterhouse had never had cause to have any professional dealings with Hubert Price, so to him, Mr Price was an unknown. He might have glimpsed him in the village but Hubert Price's face was not one committed to memory. Up until the point when Hubert Price decided to hold Constable Waterhouse captive with Reverend Smythe, Hubert Price might as well have been the man in the moon.

Constable Waterhouse told his captor that he was being very stupid and that holding one of His Majesty's Officers of the Law was an offence that was taken very seriously indeed, and that if he wanted to lessen his punishment, because he would be punished, he should release both him and the Reverend Smythe.

Price was having none of it. He wasn't a bad man, not at all but what he was doing he was doing for his family. And family always came first with Hubert Price. He was dependable but he was also weak. Not the best combination.

Reverend Smythe simply sat and took in all that was being said, but he didn't pass comment. At times he studied the bible, quietly, and at others he recited prayers from the Book of Common Prayer and the service of nine lessons and carols. He had, after all, been invited to Cambridge as a guest for the radio recording of the service.

As Jack was walking towards the ballroom, the staff manager, Mr Longfellow, came over to him. There was an urgency in his manner. 'Pardon me, sir. There's a gentleman waiting in the hall. He gave his name as Paxton, Inspector Paxton. He said that he would like a word with you.'

'Thank you, Mr Longfellow,' Jack replied and went off directly to find Paxton.

Jack found the inspector standing by the porch entrance to the hall. 'Ah, Mr France. I have something, some news which I thought you might be interested in.'

'If it's to tell me that Constable Waterhouse has disappeared, you're too late. That's what I came to notify you of earlier today. Apparently, at that time you accused me of 'rambling', as I recall.'

'Now there's no need to take that attitude, sir. But it has come to my attention that perhaps you may have been quite correct in your assumptions about criminal activity at the Old Manse; and yes, as you have just asserted, Constable Waterhouse has disappeared. He didn't call in at the station after his shift had finished, which is his custom. Sergeant Paul, who is usually on the station desk went off in search of him. Neither Waterhouse nor his bicycle have been seen since. There was no sign of anything at all at the Old Manse. We have notified Constable Waterhouse's wife, who, as you might imagine is very distressed. I thought I'd let you know that I've also asked for extra officers to be sent up to the manse to keep it discreetly under surveillance.'

'Oh no. When did you do this?'

'Just before I left to come here.'

Jack grabbed Inspector Paxton's arm. 'Come with me,' he said. And he took Paxton to where Inspector Grant was situated. 'Inspector Grant, would you mind filling in the gaps with Inspector Paxton. I have to get back to the hall.'

Grant smiled and told Paxton to take a seat in the car. Grant opened the car door and ushered Paxton inside, and then closed and locked the door of the police car. He felt it was safer that way. Whoever Paxton had dispatched, Grant felt that his own men would manage everything and anything. There was nothing to worry about.

And The Band Played On

When Jack arrived back inside Manordale he went first to see Mr Longfellow; to let him know that he was back and then Jack went straight across to the ballroom. Grainger, Arthur and Lily Graves were in their appointed places and the guests were beginning to filter through after the buffet interval. The band were setting up and would be ready to play again as soon as Jack gave the word. It was a little after nine-thirty.

This must be it, he thought, *if anything is going to happen, it will be in the next two and a half hours.* Almost as soon as the thought had entered Jack's head he was distracted by the sound of a noisy discussion going on in the hall. He turned. The voices were of a man and a woman. The man was Mr Longfellow. The woman had to be, Jack assumed, the missing accomplice.

Jack walked through to the hall and asked Mr Longfellow what the problem was. 'This lady wishes to be admitted into the ball, and I've said that she can't be, not now. I've explained that it's too late into the proceedings.'

'Leave it with me Mr Longfellow, I'll sort it out,' And Jack took the arm of the latecomer and took her over to the bar area. 'Now, may I ask you a question. Are you local to Moretondale?'

'I am, sir, lived here all my life.'

'That's all I need to know,' Jack replied, and then he said, 'Marcel, a drink for our guest.' And then he turned to the latecomer. 'What is your pleasure?' Jack asked.

'Tee total,' she said. 'Is there any lemonade?'

Jack then apologised to her and said, 'I have to go and let the band know to start playing again. When you're ready, come through to the ballroom. And I sincerely apologise for the misunderstanding earlier.' And then Jack headed to the ballroom and Arthur and Lily Graves.

Lily and Arthur were chatting when Jack approached. 'Have I missed something?' Jack asked.

'No', Lily replied. We're just making idle chatter to amuse ourselves, and, I'll just say this before you go to make your announcement, Arthur and I have had a really enjoyable evening, even with our incapacities.' Lily glanced at Arthur as she said this and he just smiled and nudged her, playfully. 'Well, I have something to say to you as well, the lady entering the ballroom now, dressed as, I suppose it could be Maid Marian, keep a close eye on her at all times. Particularly watch if she gets close to Lord and Lady Percival, or should I say the French Royalty. Notify me immediately.' Lily nodded in reply and Jack went off to the stage area to announce that the band would play again. There was applause before they started and Ambrose thanked them for that and then they began to play *Tiger Rag,* and those who could manage it, took once more to the dance floor. The ones who remained on the edge of the ballroom joined in enthusiastically every now and again with, *'Hold That Tiger'* and everyone laughed; particularly as an elephant made its way to the centre of the ballroom floor – the mahout remained feet firmly planted on the ground, in the sidelines as a spectator.

Jack was watching all the activity and chatting to his guests as and when he could, and he thought it was quite amazing that only a few people at the ball would realise they were in the middle of what would soon become a crime scene.

The Old Manse

Hubert Price heard the church clock as it struck ten and almost automatically checked his wristwatch. It was correct, to the minute.

He knew that by now his wife would be playing her part in the escapade at the ball. It would be another hour before anything happened, anything criminal. Hubert Price just hoped that neither Eileen nor her brother Richard would come to any harm. He had never wanted to be a part of this. Eileen, however, was such a stalwart, such a believer in whatever it might be that her brother said. And he had told her that this time, this time would be the last time. The last time he would have the need to do anything like this. With the money he received when the jewellery was broken up and sold he could be set for life. He would leave Moretondale, perhaps he would even leave the country. There were opportunities now in countries abroad and although it would be difficult for him to get abroad legally, he would be able to do this with help from some of the people he knew. He could change his identity and get a new passport. It was all possible. There were ways around the legalities, if you knew the right people; and he did. Richard had tried to explain all this to Eileen; she had told him that she did understand, and that her agreement to what he had in mind was forthcoming. He was her brother and she would never let him down. But there was also a more sinister side to Richard Smith. He knew that he had had always had a hold over Eileen, from the days of their childhood and that she had never been able to break the spell.

And then it was because of Eileen that Hubert agreed to his part in the scheme. Poor Hubert. Hubert too, had hoped that this would be the last time that they would ever get involved in one of Richard's unlawful activities. They had helped him as best they could over the years, but they were both older now; they could do without the worry that Richard always brought with him. Hubert just wanted the whole thing to be over. For Richard to be away from Moretondale and out of their lives, for good. He wished that he and Eileen could go safely back home to their own cottage; and no one any the wiser. They could both spin a yarn, he, and Eileen. They had had years of practice, but they both wanted a quiet life, no fuss. Hubert would be due for retirement next year, in the summer. He and Eileen had talked about it and had thought that they might spend their retirement near the sea. Perhaps Devon. They had liked it when they had had a few days' holiday there some years ago.

The clock struck half-past ten and roused Hubert Price from his reverie. He checked his wristwatch again and then looked at his two captives, Reverend Smythe and Constable Waterhouse. Waterhouse looked as though he were about to say something but then at the last minute changed his mind.

Another thought struck Hubert Price. Taking hostage a police officer just to get him out of the way was a mistake. And what for? He hadn't thought it through, he'd acted on impulse and he might live to regret it. Why on earth did he decide on a whim to bring him into the manse? Hubert recalled Eileen's words to him when he had told her what he had done; '*You fool,*' she had said, nothing more. Hubert now realised what she had meant. He had taken as a captive someone who by their very profession could put all their plans in jeopardy. Hubert Price dropped his head, *perhaps he was a fool,* he thought. And why had he done it? It was never part of the plan. The plan was to keep Reverend Smythe safely locked away while the theft at the ball was completed. Reverend Smythe would then be allowed to leave when everyone else had got safely away. And Hubert, Hubert was to keep himself hidden away until they came for him; Eileen, and Richard; and he could do that at the Old Manse. In the cellar there was a passageway, to a disused brewery. It came up on the other side of the road. The public house that had once stood there, long gone, but the rabbit warren of tunnels beneath the ground meant that you could keep well out of the way of any who might be searching for you if you knew how, and Hubert Price knew how.

The clock struck again. It was a quarter to eleven. Hubert Price looked at the two men before him and then again at Constable Waterhouse and then he felt the gun in his pocket. He knew what he had to do, but it could wait another fifteen minutes.

The Ballroom, Manordale

Jack jiggled in a sort of dance fashion across the ballroom floor to where Grainger was standing.

'Everything in hand?' Jack asked, keeping his voice low.

'Yes. If the worst happens, I will make my way out of the building,' Grainger indicated to the French Windows behind him, 'and across to the garage buildings and do my bit. Everything outside is prepared and ready'

'Thanks. It could be anytime now. It has to happen before midnight.'

The Manordale guests were enjoying themselves and at ten minutes to eleven, the French aristocracy made their way to the centre of the ballroom floor. Louis XVI bowed to his Queen and took her hand. Marie Antoinette curtsied and then they took up the hold of a popular dance of the French court, a Gavotte, much to the amusement of the onlookers. Their dance didn't fit with the music, but it was lively and they were determined to put on a good show. After a few moments the pair separated their hold and upped their tempo again to be in time with the rag being played. There was then uproarious laughter from the other dancers on the floor and those onlookers standing by the edge of the ballroom. Lily was keenly watching, to see if she could get Maid Marian in her sights. When Lily eventually caught sight of her, Maid Marian was in deep conversation with someone dressed as a mediaeval pedlar. Their voices were low and would never have been heard above the sound of the music, anyway. Lily thought that Maid Marian looked slightly put out but then Lily saw her nodding her head frantically while the pedlar carried on talking. The pedlar was obviously an important part of whatever it was that was going to happen.

The pedlar's costume was of the traditional mediaeval style and the coat had large pockets. In front of him, the pedlar carried a tray on which were placed a few pots and trinkets and a small copper kettle. The tray was kept secure by a leather strap that went around the pedlar's neck. Lily assumed the pedlar was a man, judging by the type of shoes that were worn, but she wasn't really sure. She nudged Arthur, and gestured towards the two partygoers, but didn't point, so as not to draw any unwanted attention.

A few people had decided to take a break from the dancing, leaving the floor to those of a more energetic persuasion. Jack was mingling with those guests who were taking a breather. Briefly chatting to each couple or singleton before moving on. Everything had to be seen to appear normal.

Jack then moved towards Lily and Arthur Graves. He spoke briefly to Lily.

Maid Marian and the pedlar were still on the dance floor although now Maid Marian had a look of consternation on her face.

Louis XVI and Marie Antoinette were still dancing very energetically, much to the delight of those watching. The pearl brooch and the diamond tiara of the French Queen looked spectacular as the couple danced about the floor The stones were catching the light and causing a rainbow effect to be cast about the walls of the ballroom.

The elephant, who was still on the dance floor was swinging its trunk in time to the music and making a good fist of it.

Jack glanced down at his wristwatch. It was one minute to eleven. Almost simultaneously, Maid Marian moved quickly from the dance floor, and out into the hall, rushing past Mr Longfellow, who was taken by surprise. Maid Marian knew where she was heading and once she had flicked a switch in the entrance hall to douse the lights, she ran out of the building and into the grounds of Manordale.

On the dance floor, the pedlar moved quickly towards Lady Percival. The lights were out. There was confusion and Lady Percival felt a tug at her costume, she moved her hands up and then felt at where the brooch had been. It was gone. Her hand moved to her head. There was no tiara. A moment later and the light was restored, and Grainger returned to the ballroom. The pedlar was already heading to the door of the ballroom and towards the entrance hall and the exit from Manordale. He was quick but not as quick as Arthur Graves, who, as the pedlar approached grabbed the pedlar's leg with the crook of his walking stick.

The pedlar tripped and lay sprawled across the ballroom floor. He was surrounded by guests and one of them, the mahout, removed the mask from the now prostrate, pedlar.

'It's Richard Smith,' someone called from the crowd, and as those gathered turned to see who it was that had called out, the woman in question removed her mask. It was Mrs Hindmarsh, she continued, 'And to think, I said that I didn't think I'd recognise him again, too many years have gone by. But it is most certainly him. It is Richard Smith,' she said, her voice almost trailing to nothing as she spoke.

Two men came forward and held Richard Smith down. In another second Inspector Grant came into Manordale. He had a constable with him, who had handcuffed Eileen Price in his charge. When she saw her brother, she said, almost in tears, 'I'm sorry, Richard. I tried.'

Her brother said nothing.

Two more officers entered the ballroom to assist with the apprehension of the two in their custody. There were other police officers, Jack noticed, in the entrance hall.

Ambrose and his band had stopped playing. The revelry of a few minutes earlier had subsided. The guests were now in a state of shock and disbelief. Jack looked at Inspector Grant, 'If you don't mind, Inspector, I'd like to say a few words to my guests.'

Jack explained briefly why everything had had to go ahead, why the Manordale ball had to be as it had been in years past. There were nods of agreement, and something that Jack found quite amusing, in a charming way, a spontaneous round of applause from everyone inside Manordale.

Then it was time for Inspector Grant to speak. He did so as Eileen Price and Richard Smith were being led away for questioning.

'Ladies and gentlemen, can I have your attention, just for a few minutes. Mr Jack France, your host, informed me of some strange incidents around the village and it is thanks to him and his way of not letting obstacles get in his way but of determinedly carrying on regardless in his pursuit of truth and justice that we have been able to apprehend the guilty parties involved, here tonight, at the Manordale Ball. Mr France was correct in his assumption that this was where an incident would take place. I have to say to you all that I hope we didn't spoil the proceedings too much, and to the French Royalty who were in attendance tonight, we hope to return the stolen items to you as soon as possible. Thanks to you all. Have a Happy Christmas, and I'll leave you now to carry on. Goodnight.' There was a slight pause and then Inspector Grant said, 'And Mr France, could you join me outside, as soon as you are able?' Jack nodded by way of reply.

When Inspector Grant had left Manordale, Jack took the floor again. He said that he was sorry if any distress had been caused to any of his guests. It wasn't his intention to upset them but it had been done as Inspector Grant had just said, to bring criminals to justice. There were cheers. No one disagreed with Jack France's motives.

All that was left, was for Jack to now draw proceedings to a close. His guests understood. He paid special thanks to all his staff, particularly Grainger, and Arthur and Lily Graves. Jack thanked Ambrose and his band and Marcel, the cocktail waiter for the evening and said that he hoped they would be coming back to Manordale soon. He apologised to all the guests and staff for the untimely ending of the ball and then he said that he hoped that everyone would understand as he would have to leave them now as Inspector Grant had asked to speak with him.

Grant was outside waiting for Jack to join him. 'I'm off to the Old Manse now,' Grant said, 'my men are going to get inside. Are you coming with us? You won't be allowed into the property as it's in the hands of the police now, but you can come along as an observer.'
    'I'll come,' Jack replied.

At the manse, the three inhabitants had heard the church clock chiming the half hour. Only one amongst them knew the significance of this. Hubert Price knew that the caper at the Manordale ball would, by now have been completed. Whether it had been successful or not he didn't know, but he hoped that it had. For the sake of all his family. He wanted this night to be over. He wanted to be away from this place for good.
    The captives seemed to be dozing. They had no idea why they were being held, but they too, wanted it

to be over. Suddenly, there was the sound of banging on the door of the manse and light seemed to illuminate the inside of the room they were in. Then they heard the sirens and the loud hailer. They were not in need of sleep anymore. They felt refreshed. The police were outside. They were going to get out. They were safe. Constable Waterhouse and Reverend Smythe looked at their captor. 'I think it's over now,' Waterhouse said, 'time to give up. You haven't harmed us; the courts will be lenient with you.'

'I haven't harmed you but I've done other things. Other things I'd rather not tell anyone about and it was all because of Eileen's brother, Richard. He was bad from the day he was born but my Eileen, she thought the world of him.'

Footsteps were heard on the stairs and the door suddenly burst open. 'Time to give up, now. Come on, let's go quietly,' Inspector Grant said. Price looked at the Inspector. 'I'm not going. I'm not going anywhere.'

'Yes you are. You're coming with us. Come on. Let's get this over with.'

'No I'm not,' Price said, and he took the gun from his jacket pocket, waving it towards Waterhouse and Reverend Smythe as he did.

'No!' Grant said. 'Don't do anything you'd regret. Don't be silly, put the gun down and come over here to me. We don't want to add a murder to the list. And you know what a murder would mean, don't you?'

Price waved the gun about again; and again the Inspector told him to put the gun down.

Price turned to face the Inspector. 'I'm not going anywhere. I'm not going to do anything I'll regret.' And Price looked Inspector Grant in the face and then held the gun to his forehead and pulled the trigger. Hubert Price was dead.

A man was dead but Constable Waterhouse and Reverend Smythe were relieved to be free and to walk down the stairs and out into the grounds of the Old Manse and into the fresh air. Jack went over and had a brief word with them both before they were taken to a waiting police car and driven over to Melford where they would make statements.

The manse was searched, but as those involved had first thought, there was no one else at the property.

Inspector Paxton had been brought across to the manse and for a while was in discussion with Inspector Grant. Afterwards, Paxton felt duty bound to give his sincere apologies to Jack France. Jack accepted, and Paxton left the scene. Jack thought that Paxton would be pleased to get home and leave the events of the last twenty-four hours behind him.

Jack waited on the sidelines and eventually Grant came over to speak with him. 'I'm pleased for your help with this case, Mr France, and for pointing us in the right direction. It would have been more difficult for us; had you cancelled the Manordale ball.'

'That was something that could never have happened,' Jack replied, And then he asked, 'The shot that was fired, was someone injured? I've only seen Constable Waterhouse and Reverend Smythe leave the building.'

'A death, I'm afraid, Mr France. It was I believe, Hubert Price, you perhaps knew him?'

'Indeed. His wife Eileen was the churchwarden at St. Stephen's, and as now appears, an accomplice to her brother, Richard. I'd no idea about Mr Price, though. He was always a gentle soul. Enjoyed spending time on his allotment.'

'Mm. There's more to his story than there would seem at first sight. I suspect he was under the thumb of his wife.'

At first Jack didn't say anything and then said only, 'I see,' in reply.

'Are you back off to Manordale, now sir?'

'Yes. I'll walk. It will seem quite pleasant. I think there might be a frost on the way.'

'Safe journey, and we may have to be in touch with you over the next few days. We may have some questions for you.'

'I understand. Goodnight Inspector Grant.' And Jack turned and walked off in the direction of Manordale and home.'

It was strange walking into Manordale. It was now Christmas Eve but such a lot had happened over the last few days and it seemed as if time had, in a way, stood still while the culprits of a planned crime, were caught and then both, in time, would be able to be brought to justice and face the consequences for their actions.

Ambrose and his band along with Marcel had left and they were no doubt on their way back to London. The guests had gone and would have stories to relate to their friends and family over the coming days and weeks about what might happen in a sleepy village around Christmas time.

The extra staff had left and the catering staff had also gone, except for Mr Jarvis and Mr Longfellow, who thought that they should both wait at the hall until Mr France returned. Jack thanked them for their consideration and then asked them if they liked whisky. 'I'm rather partial to the odd glass in the evening,' Mr Jarvis replied, and Mr Longfellow agreed that he too was of the same persuasion. Jack walked into his study and took a couple of bottles from his 'supply'. He handed a bottle to each of the men who accepted their gifts gratefully and thanked Mr France for his generosity. As the men left the house, Jack locked the doors of Manordale and went across to the ballroom. It was completely empty. Jack walked to the sitting room and found the rest of his staff and guests there, Grainger, Lily and Arthur Graves, Miss Esther Abingdon, Miss Susan Packham and Miss Waterstone.

As he walked into the room, Jack looked at the faces before him and said, 'Well, what a night.'

Jack had a few questions he needed to ask and paused for a moment while he decided what to do. His decision reached, he began, 'I just have to ask, I left pretty much as Eileen Price and Richard Smith, were being taken away; did they take that they had been caught, in their stride as it were. There was no commotion?'

'Richard Smith was fairly resigned, I thought,' Grainger said,' but Eileen Price was screaming, saying that her Hubert had caused the trouble, that he was nothing but a fool.'

'He was a quiet man,' Jack replied, 'and I hope Eileen Price will find it in her heart to forgive him.'

'She will,' Lily said.

'I hope so. Hubert Price is dead. He shot himself at close range. I'm sorry to have to blurt it out like this, but it's the truth, nonetheless,' Jack said.

Gasps were audible in the small space of the sitting room. 'I have left you with a lot to digest;' then Jack asked, ' Lord and Lady Percival, were they able to get home safely?'

Grainger again answered, 'Yes. They were taken home by the police. Lady Percival was upset about it all, especially as up until then it had been a very enjoyable evening. Their car is on the drive. Brindle, the Percival's chauffeur will come over for it in the morning.'

'And their jewellery, Lady Percival's jewellery, it was in Richard Smith's possession?'

'Yes. In the little copper kettle,' Miss Abingdon said. 'How amazing to go to all that trouble, and the fiddling with the lights, as well. It was all planned to the last detail.'

'Almost.' Jack said.

'That's a telling word. A word that holds more than it's given to,' Susan said.

'You are correct. But I'll leave that tale for tomorrow, over breakfast.'

'Oh, can't you say anything now?' Lily asked.

'I'm afraid not; and truth be told, I'm too tired to be bothered, but one last task I will fulfil will be to make sure you and Arthur get to your cottage safely.'

'I can wheel the chair if you want,' Grainger offered.

'If you're sure it's no trouble,' Jack said.

'None at all, sir'.

'Thanks for that. I'll see you to the door and I'll lock up the main doors to the hall. Jarvis and Longfellow have both left now. There will be a police presence here tonight, in the grounds and at the Old Manse, so we can all sleep safely in our beds. I think we might all need a good rest.'

Goodnights and thanks were said and the parties separated. Jack returned to the sitting room.

'And that's it?' Miss Waterstone said.

'That's it. The house is secured for the night. Please, excuse me and I wish you all a good night's sleep and I will see you in the dining room tomorrow morning, or should I say, later this morning. Goodnight, all.' And Jack France left the sitting room and climbed the stairs of Manordale. He was tired and he couldn't hide it any longer. He knew that he would be asleep as soon as his head touched the pillow.

Christmas Eve

The day was bright with a sharp frost. Jack looked out of his bedroom window and out across the landscape that was Manordale. The scene he looked down on was Christmas card, picture-perfect. It filled him with a sense of well-being, and for that he was glad.

At a little before eight o'clock he joined his guests in the dining room.

The sideboard was laid out with everything a *Manordale* English breakfast was known for. And it was apparent that Mrs Hindmarsh was at the reins as there were devilled kidneys. Not to everyone's taste but definitely to Jack's.

'Mr France, come on and sit with us,' Esther Abingdon said, 'and do tell us all about the story from last night. We want all the news. Every single detail.'

'When I've eaten these kidneys, and have finished my tea, then I'll bring you up to date with all the facts, as I have them.'

All the while he was eating, Jack could feel the eyes of his guests upon him. It didn't make him hurry his food; he was never one for that but it did make him realise that he perhaps should not tease his guests. What had happened after all, was deadly serious.

Jack pushed his plate to one side and got up and went to pour himself a cup of tea. 'Any takers?' he asked, 'while I'm here.'

Esther blurted out, 'No. We just want you to come and sit down and tell us your story.'

'There isn't really that much more to tell. I had my concerns when I saw the Old Manse boarded up but after checking with various people I couldn't really see why I should have any doubts and tried to push everything to one side; but then you see all the explanations I was given were never complete. I couldn't let it drop. I had a gut feeling and it wasn't leaving me. I kept returning to the manse to check the grounds and also to see if there was any sign of life. There wasn't, but it didn't deter me. In fact, it made me all the more inquisitive. And then I reread a letter I'd received from the diocese informing me of the new incumbent. The letter had lain on my desk for a day or two after first reading and so I was, you might say, late to the news, although all of Moretondale seemed to know of Reverend Smythe's arrival anyway. And then, because I'd been told of his arrival by so many people in Moretondale, that was the detail that was in my head, not what was said in the letter from the diocese.'

'And how did you know Richard Smith wasn't the real vicar?' Susan asked.

'It was his shoes. I called on Eileen Price to see if she knew anything about the Old Manse. She didn't but she had a visitor and she introduced him to me as Reverend Smythe. Everything was very pleasant and we chatted but then I noticed Reverend Smythe's shoes. They were brown. They should have been black, and that one tiny point made me dubious as to his identity. I went along with it, though. I didn't want anyone to know of my suspicions. At that point in time I didn't realise that he and Eileen Price were in cahoots, as it were.'

'But where was the actual Reverend Smythe all this time. You said you knew the date of his arrival?' Esther said.

'Yes, the date of his arrival, the 23rd of December, that was when Reverend Smythe was due to visit Moretondale and introduce himself to me, but as I said with all I was being told in the village the date had slipped my mind completely. Abysmal of me really, but there we are. As for where he was, that was something I had to find out. I telephoned a friend of mine, Sir Cecil Brookes. He did some ferreting about and got back to me. Reverend Smythe had been reported as missing.'

There were gasps as the story was related and eventually Jack reached the point in his tale where he said that he was certain that Reverend Smythe must be being held against his will at the Old Manse. He told them that Paxton had sent a constable along from Melford to discreetly keep an eye on the property and that as they may or may not have known, eventually he too, was taken hostage and held in the manse.

Jack continued, 'The ball had to go ahead. I knew that whatever was going to happen would happen at the ball.'

'And the lights?' Esther asked, how did you get the lights back on so quickly?'

'My chauffeur, Grainger had everything under control. We had a plan of possibilities. The lights going off was one of those possibilities and Grainger knew how and when to respond. And you saw how Arthur, my butler brought his walking stick into play, to bring the culprit down?'

'He was very good,' Miss Waterstone said. 'And while he was confined to a wheelchair. Remarkable.'

'Yes. My staff are remarkable. And there we are. Up to date and I may have to leave you for an hour or so shortly, as I want to go across to Wrendale and see how Lord and Lady Percival are. When are you expecting to be leaving Esther?'

'Well, that's just it. Would you mind awfully if I stayed until the new year? There isn't a train today and nothing until the 27th of December and Susan, Miss Waterstone and myself are all getting along famously, so Jack, would you mind?'

'You haven't any other devious reasons for this, have you? You haven't a Henry Wilde hidden away somewhere, have you?'

There was laughter from the gathered party, and then Jack said, 'Well, why not? Yes Esther, I would be delighted to have your company over Christmas.'

Esther got up from her chair and went over to Jack. She looked at him and said, 'It really is good to have friends. Thank you.'

Later That Morning

Jack had Grainger drive him across to Wrendale. He didn't want too much time to elapse before he caught up with the Percivals. He wanted to set his own mind at rest, as well as theirs. Lord Percival greeted Jack as he came into the house. 'Good morning to you, Jack. I say. What an enjoyable ball last night. Kicks everything else over Christmas into a cocked hat. Come in and sit down. Mary's been so anxious for you to call over so that she can thank you herself.' Lord Percival ushered Jack through to the morning-room. Lady Percival was sitting by the window. 'The frost is so Christmassy, don't you think?' she said. Jack smiled. 'The same thought struck me this morning,' he said.

Jack and Lord Percival took a seat. A maid came in to see if any refreshments were required. Lady Percival asked for a pot each of tea and coffee and whatever there might be to go with it. 'Now Jack, I hope I behaved exactly as French Royalty might, last night. I've never enjoyed myself so much in a long time. What a hoot! And the lights going off and then coming on and the police and Eileen Price, who'd have thought it? And, the pedlar, who we now know as her brother, getting hooked in Arthur's walking stick. It was better than a book, and John and I were in it. And one more thing, Ambrose, and his band. How did you manage to pull that one off?'

'State secret, I'm afraid. Except it's not. I mentioned didn't I, that I have friends in London,' Jack answered. And then added, 'I'm pleased that you have both taken it so well. I thought I might be suddenly off your Christmas card list for future years.'

Mary Percival laughed. 'We might have to send you two next year.'

'Lord Percival looked at Jack, 'The men being held in the manse, they were safe?'

'The captives were all safe, thankfully. It was Constable Waterhouse and our new vicar, Reverend Smythe. I expect they're taking it easy this morning. And I have to find out if the new vicar will still be joining us after this escapade. We could have put him off.'

'I doubt it Jack. And, what I've heard, is it true, that Hubert Price died?' Lord Percival asked.

'Very true, I'm afraid. He shot himself. A nasty business for everyone. But I'm pleased you recovered your jewellery, Lady Mary. It was in the small copper kettle, I believe?'

'Yes. And they've been returned to me no more than half an hour ago,' Lady Mary said, and then reached across to a table where the brooch and diamond tiara had been placed. She scooped them up together in her hand. 'All that trouble and death for these,' she said. And she held aloft the items before returning them to the table. Jack watched her, and then she smiled and continued, 'And they are paste. That's the only reason they come out every year for the ball. I know the rumour around the village is that they're genuine, but they're not. Most definitely not.'

Jack flashed Lady Mary a bemused look which she returned with a Mona Lisa like smile.

There was a knock on the door. And when the door opened it was the maid with a tray of refreshments. 'We'll serve ourselves,' Lady Mary said, and with no more ado, the maid left the room.

An hour later and Jack was back at Manordale. It felt good to be home. His guests were in the sitting room. He could hear their easy conversation and was thankful that the 'almost strangers' got on so well, like friends. He went through and joined them. 'The Percival's are fine,' he said, as he sat down in an armchair.

'That's good,' Esther said, 'and there's been a message left for you. Only ten or fifteen minutes after you'd left. It was Reverend Smythe. He called by to see you.'

Jack chipped in, 'Good news or bad?'

'We think it's good. The carol service at St. Stephen's. It will go ahead. And he will lead the service. He said it was easier for him to stay here than try and get to Cambridge for the recording. He's booked himself in to stay at the *Ring o' Bells*. Everything's ready, so, six o' clock this evening.'

'That's a relief,' Jack replied. 'We must have made a good impression or something.'

Notes from the Author

Thank you for reading the third book in the Jack France Mysteries. I hope you have enjoyed your *Christmas at Manordale.*

If you would like to leave a review for the book, you can do this on ***Amazon*** or ***Goodreads.***

The next *Jack France Mystery*, **Murder in Budapest** will be out in 2024.

If you would like to check my website for news, competitions, events, and author visits, please visit:
        https://mgth13.wixsite.com/margaretholbrook

    You can also *follow me on* Bookbub
Thank you!
M. H.

Author's Notes

There's always a lot of research to be done with these books and that's part of the fun and because of that here are some facts, and recipes for cocktails. Enjoy.

Ambrose and his band did play at the May Fair hotel in the 1920s and were indeed very popular.

Bert Ambrose was born in 1896 and died in 1971. He played at the May Fair hotel from its opening in 1927 until 1940. He had a flat at the hotel that he lived in, even when he had finished his playing there.

When his music style declined in popularity with the public, he became a manager and in 1958 discovered the singer, Kathy Kirby.

While at a recording with Kirby for Yorkshire Television, Ambrose collapsed, and died later in Leeds Infirmary.

(Notes from London Remembers)

The Service of Nine Lessons and Carols

The first time the service of nine lessons and carols was heard at King's College Chapel, Cambridge was in 1918.

The service of nine lessons and carols was first introduced by the Dean of King's College, Cambridge, Eric Milner White.

The service itself, however, was first devised by the first Bishop of Truro, Edward White Benson in 1880. (This was before the cathedral was built).

The first BBC Radio broadcast of the service from King's College Chapel, Cambridge, took place in December 1928.

BBC Archive

And now for those cocktails served at the Manordale Ball.

Martini   *This is for a dry martini*

Ingredients

60ml gin, 1 tbsp dry vermouth, few ice cubes, olive to garnish

Stir together gin, vermouth and ice, strain and serve into a martini glass, and garnish with olive on a cocktail stick. My favourite!

Gimlet

Ingredients

50ml lime cordial (Roses or any of choice) 50ml dry gin, few ice cubes, lime slice to garnish

Stir together in a jug the lime cordial, gin and ice cubes. Strain the mixture into a chilled glass and garnish with lemon slice.

Coconut Champagne Punch

Ingredients

1 750ml bottle of inexpensive Champagne or Cava, 17.5 fl oz coconut water 4fl oz Pineapple or Orange juice. Assorted fruit pieces, pineapple, strawberries, raspberries.

Put all fruit pieces onto a skewer and if time, place in a freezer for one hour prior to serving.

Mix in a jug the coconut milk and fruit juice. Pour into tall glasses leaving a space at the top. Put in chilled fruit skewers, (like a straw) and top up the glass with Champagne.

And a Mrs Hindmarsh Special, Devilled Kidneys

Ingredients

1 Lamb's kidney per person, roughly chopped
2 shallots or 1 small onion finely chopped
A little oil for frying

For the sauce:
A dash of sherry, apple vinegar,
1tsp redcurrant jelly,
1tbsp tomato puree
Worcestershire sauce, English mustard, salt and cayenne pepper to taste
small carton 3-4 fl oz of double or single cream

Method

Make sure the core is removed from the kidneys

Add small amount of oil to frying pan and add chopped onions and brown lightly. Add the chopped kidneys when the oil is HOT and cook for one-two minutes, *stirring continuously until the kidneys are lightly browned.*

To the kidneys and onions add a dash of sherry, dash of apple vinegar and 1 tsp redcurrant jelly. Stir well until blended. Add a couple of shakes of Worcestershire sauce, English mustard, salt and cayenne pepper and tomato puree. Mix well. Add cream and mix until blended. Cook for about two minutes until the sauce bubbles. Ensure the kidneys are cooked through.

If you don't fancy kidneys use other meat or perhaps meat substitutes.

Serve with other traditional English breakfast foods as a breakfast dish or on toast for a lunch or supper dish.

I don't eat cream and omit it from the recipe.

You can add, (to replace the cream if you wish) extra tomato puree, and a splash of water to slacken the sauce if desired.
M.H.

ABOUT THE AUTHOR

Margaret Holbrook grew up in Cheshire where she still lives. Her work has been published in anthologies and magazines and broadcast on radio.

She writes fiction, plays and poetry.
In 2014 her play *The Supper Party* was a finalist in the 'Grand Words' competition, run in conjunction with the *Grand Theatre,* Blackpool.

Her short story, *Our Brian* was longlisted for the BBC Radio 4 programme, 'Opening Lines', in the same year.

In 2015 her play *Sandy's Ashes* was performed at Congleton festival and in November 2015 her short story *Pig Man* was shortlisted for the Cheshire Prize Literature and is published in the Cheshire Prize Anthology, *Patches of Light.*

In 2017 her play Ruthless was longlisted for the Top Five Competition at Bolton's *Octagon Theatre.*

In 2021 her play *The Bus Stop* was performed at Buxton Festival Fringe after a short Northwest Tour in 2019.

In 2022 her play *Any Other Day* was performed at Buxton Festival Fringe. It is set in the garden of the Wilmslow home of Alan Turing a few days after his death.

Acknowledgements

*My very special thanks go to Miss Susan Packham who entered the draw to be a character in *Christmas at Manordale*. I hope Susan enjoys the part she plays in the story.

Also, thanks to Mr Sam Ford for agreeing to do the draw and revealing the winner. He didn't know he was going to be asked until he arrived at the door with my Rington's tea delivery!

Printed in Great Britain
by Amazon

31970372R00129